A CHRISTMAS AT HIGHBURY

OTHER BOOKS BY MICHELLE COX:

A Girl Like You

A Ring of Truth

A Promise Given

A Veil Removed

A Child Lost

A Spying Eye

A Haunting at Linley

The Fallen Woman's Daughter

Matched in Merriweather

A CHRISTMAS AT HIGHBURY

A HENRIETTA AND INSPECTOR HOWARD NOVELLA

MICHELLE COX

Ebook ISBN: 979-8-9880097-5-7
Paperback ISBN: 979-8-9880097-4-0

Library of Congress Control Number: 2024919690

DEDICATION

Marcia Marie Martino
Not just a sister, but a best friend. Thank you for your enthusiastic encouragement, gentle suggestions, and, most especially, your listening ear.

It has always meant the world to me.

"For it is good to be children sometimes, and never better than at Christmas, when its mighty Founder was a child Himself."

—CHARLES DICKENS

CHAPTER 1

Henrietta took a deep breath as the Rolls pulled up in front of Highbury. Teddy lay cuddled in her arms, thankfully asleep after the long drive up from Chicago.

The palatial mansion in Winnetka, Clive's boyhood home, looked just as she remembered it, and for a moment it seemed as if they had been gone only a few days and not over a year! She peered out the car window at the massive stone mansion, the front windows of which were now draped in lush evergreen roping in anticipation of Christmas, a bright-red bow in the middle of each. Despite the cheery décor, however, and the fact that she was not returning as Clive's formerly impoverished bride but rather as Lady Linley, it was hard not to feel at least a little intimidated.

"Do you want me to take him, miss?" Edna asked from where she sat perched across from her in a sort of interior rumble seat, British style, which was perfect for a child or, say, a servant. "Miss," of course, was not really the correct title with which to address Lady Linley, but Edna had a terrible habit of forgetting such things.

"No, I've got him," Henrietta said, though Teddy *was* getting a little bit heavy. She glanced over at Clive, who was looking at her appreciatively. He wouldn't say it, of course, but she knew he was eager to show off their little prince: Montague Alcott Linley Theodore, not only the future Lord Linley but also heir to Highbury and the Howard fortune.

"Well, then let me put a blanket over him," Edna said, producing one from somewhere on her person. "He's not used to this cold. Don't want him to freeze in this weather."

"I hardly think he'll freeze from the car to the house." Henrietta began shifting herself forward, as she could see Albert, the footman, already hurrying down the front steps to open the car doors. "Anyone would think you've lived in London your whole life, Edna."

"Seems like it, though, don't it, Pascal?" Edna asked of the young man seated in the front seat beside Fritz.

"Well, *non*, not *exactement*," Pascal answered with only a slight turn of his head toward the backseat. His eyes were instead glued to the large house and grounds in front of them. It was a look the Howards were growing used to by now, as Pascal seemed amazed by almost everything they encountered from the moment they had disembarked in New York. Clive and Henrietta had first met the former groomsman on a case in Strasbourg, and he had stuck, becoming not only Clive's valet, for lack of a better available position, but more importantly, Edna's husband. He now held the rank of head butler in their London townhouse, though, in truth, he was much too young and inexperienced for such a role. But he was a fast learner and ridiculously faithful. Henrietta could only imagine what Billings would say about him in the servants' hall.

The door of the Rolls opened then, letting in a gust of cold air. Edna hopped out and stood by eagerly while Albert held the car door for Henrietta, still carefully holding Teddy, as she began to inch out. Clive, meanwhile, having swiftly exited from his side, hurried over and put his arm sturdily around Henrietta, as if she and Teddy needed steadying—or, God forbid, protecting. His previous obsessive desire to protect her from, well, everything—criminal elements, illness, even the weather—had unfortunately expanded now to include his son.

Seeing her mistress secured, Edna joined Pascal and the flood of other servants swarming now from the house to unpack the bags from the trunk. Edna tucked one under each arm, picked up a third, and began shuffling toward the service entrance.

"Edna!" Henrietta called from halfway up the front stone steps. "Where are you going? This way." She looked pointedly at Clive for support, who likewise called out.

"Yes, Pascal. This way."

Edna hesitated, set her bags down, and scurried back. "If you please, miss, it will be better this way. If we don't, we won't half hear it from this lot the whole time we're here." She tilted her head toward the service entrance. "Give me two shakes, and I'll be upstairs in a jiffy gettin' all settled. Don't you worry."

Henrietta was about to protest further, but she was eager to get Teddy out of the biting wind. "All right, then, but remember what we talked about."

Edna gave a brief nod and then hurried back to where Pascal was waiting, the collar of his coat turned up over his ears.

Together, Clive and Henrietta climbed the massive stone steps, Clive's arm still protectively around her, though the steps weren't the least bit slippery. Indeed, no snow had yet fallen, despite the proximity to Christmas, which was unusual for Chicago at this time of year. It rarely snowed in London, and it was one of the things that Henrietta was hoping to see on this trip back.

Billings stood, his face unmoving, at attention at the door. He gave a stiff bow. "Welcome home, your lordship, my lady," he said in his slow, nasally way, though he did not look directly at them and instead fixed his droopy eyes on the opposite doorframe.

"Hello, Billings." Clive clapped the butler on the shoulder. "You can drop all the lordship nonsense, though," he said, unbuttoning his coat.

"Yes, m'lord."

"Oh! You've arrived!" exclaimed Antonia. "Sidney!" she called behind her. "They're here! Oh, let me see him!" Antonia Howard rushed forward and immediately peeled back Teddy's blanket. The baby's eyes flickered open and his little brow furrowed. Instinctively, he jerked a tiny fist toward his mouth.

"Oh, Clive!" Antonia gushed. "He looks just like you!"

Sidney Bennett entered the room, smiling broadly, and held out his hand to Clive. "You've made it, old boy. Well done. How was the voyage?"

"A little choppy at times, but overall fine." Clive allowed Billings, who had obsequiously stepped forward, to peel off his coat. "I suppose congratulations are in order," Clive said formally, looking from Sidney to his mother.

Clive had insisted often enough that his mother's somewhat hasty marriage to his late father's right-hand man of business was an arrangement that he approved of, but Henrietta wasn't so sure. She and Clive had been too absorbed with their own affairs in England of late to care much at the time, but now that the two men were face-to-face in his father's house, Clive seemed a bit cool. Henrietta shifted Teddy and hoped that Clive would set aside any ill will for the sake of Christmas. But one never knew.

"Thank you," Sidney said genuinely, his smile broad. He gingerly approached Henrietta and kissed her on the cheek. "You're looking well, Henrietta." His voice was soft and kind, as Sidney had ever been. "And this must be the heir apparent." He shifted his gaze to the little man in her arms.

Henrietta tried turning Teddy a bit so that they could see him better. His big blue eyes were large as he looked around the unfamiliar place, his gaze locking on the golden chandelier above them, his fist firmly in his mouth now.

"Yes, here he is!" Henrietta beamed. "Would you like to hold him, Antonia?"

"Hold him? Heavens, no! I'm sure he needs changing and feeding and cleaning and who knows what else. Bridget here will take him up to the nursery until your servants can get unpacked." With a nod of her head toward a maid standing at attention in the corner, the young woman hurried forward and gave a light curtsey.

"Oh, no; that won't be necessary," Henrietta said, though the girl seemed unsure if she was referring to the curtsey or taking the baby. She took a step back and looked confusedly at Antonia.

Henrietta slightly twisted her body away from the maid and gripped Teddy tighter. "Do you have us in our old wing?" she asked Antonia.

"Yes, I've had the east wing reopened for you and Clive, but little Montague will of course be up in the nursery on the third floor. You needn't worry," she said in response to Henrietta's instant frown. "Nanny will see to him." She gave Bridget another stern nod, and the young woman again approached.

Henrietta gritted her teeth. She had known it was going to be this way; she and Clive had discussed it ahead of time and had agreed that they would stand together against what was sure to be Antonia's tyranny regarding the baby and any number of other things. But this was an easier proposition for Clive, who was used to standing up to his mother and seemed unaffected by any guilt she tried to lob on him. Henrietta, on the other hand, found it difficult to so easily dismiss her. Though she was now Lady Linley and the head of her own household in London, not to mention an officer on the boards of many worthy London charities, she still quaked a little in front of her one-time nemesis.

But that wasn't exactly true, Henrietta admitted, letting out a little sigh. Antonia had never really been a *nemesis*, though she *had* made things a little difficult for her when Clive had introduced her as his intended. To be fair, Henrietta knew that Antonia had since accepted her, even loved her, but she could still be rather trying in certain circumstances. She was used to getting her own way.

"Well, since I'm still nursing him, Antonia," Henrietta announced, her chin jutting out just a little, "it has to be me who feeds him. I'm sure you'll understand that. And also why he needs to be in the east wing with us. You needn't worry," she said hurriedly, noting Antonia's already-open mouth of protest. "We can just have a cradle brought down from the nursery and placed in our room."

Antonia's face darkened. "Nursing him! Dear me!" She looked accusatorily at Clive, as if this were *his* fault. "How very antiquated! And you call *me* the one stuck in the past!" She glanced at Sidney for confirmation, but he just smiled wanly. "I'd have thought the two of you would be more modern in your approach. In my day, we employed a wet nurse. Didn't seem to hurt Clive or Julia one bit," she tsked. "Have you not thought to wean him? He's already seven months!"

Henrietta threw a weary glance at Clive, who responded immediately. "Mother, we're still quite tired from the journey. Let us go upstairs and get settled and changed and then we'll join you and Sidney for a drink in the drawing room."

"Capital idea, Clive," Sidney agreed. "Do take your time."

"Yes, all right," Antonia said disapprovingly. "But I don't expect you'll get a minute of sleep."

Bridget gave her mistress a final questioning look, and Antonia dismissed her with a quick tilt of her head. Silently, the young woman retreated. Henrietta shifted Teddy onto one hip and crossed the black-and-white checkerboard tiles of the foyer toward the grand staircase, which was also bedecked with evergreen roping looped through the cherry spindles.

"The house looks beautiful, Mother." Clive kissed Antonia on the cheek and followed Henrietta up the stairs. "Oh, and Mother, we call him Teddy," Clive called down over the railing.

"Teddy? Whatever for?"

"Well, Theodore *is* one of his names. The same, I might remind you, as your father's."

"Oh, Clive! But Teddy is so very common. If you must call him something, why not Monty?" she called up.

"We'll be down shortly, Mother."

Henrietta let out a little groan as they hurried down the upstairs hallway. Teddy was beginning to fuss now; he was surely hungry.

"Well, that went about as well as expected," Clive said with a crimped grin as they passed various priceless portraits and landscapes that lined both walls. His father's art collection was immense.

"Did it?" Henrietta asked wryly, shifting Teddy onto her shoulder now. He had started to cry. "I didn't notice."

"Darling, we knew it was going to be difficult. Give it time. And remember, it's Christmas."

"Funny. I was going to say the very same to you."

"Oh? To what exactly are you referring?" Clive hurried ahead to open the large walnut pocket doors at the end of the hallway that marked the beginning of the east wing. "Please don't tell me it's regarding some imagined hurt toward Pascal. I can assure you, darling, he's really more robust than you give him credit for."

"I was referring, you rude thing, to your rather cool reception of poor Sidney," she said over Teddy's cries as she hurried through their private sitting room and on into her bedroom, which, of course, Clive shared, though he had his own on the other side of the wing.

Edna was already there, thankfully, unpacking the open cases strewn across the massive four-poster bed. She put down the gown she was holding. "Oh, there you are, miss! I was wondering when you'd get up here. I can't believe he's made it this long. Well past his feeding time." Edna pulled a rocking chair out of the corner and took the now wailing Teddy while Henrietta shrugged out of her coat and let it drop onto the floor as she began to fumble with her buttons.

Clive cleared his throat. "I'll see that Pascal brings the cradle down," he said and quickly ducked back out of the room.

Henrietta sat down in the rocker near the fire and took Teddy back in her arms, arranging him at her breast until he latched on and began sucking hungrily. Clive, while trying to adopt modernity, still struggled with certain aspects of fatherhood, one of them being watching his son nurse, which he thought should be done in the strictest confines of privacy. Henrietta forgave him this peculiarity, knowing as she did that he was trying his hardest to be a good father. He made it a point, for example, to hold Teddy each day, which, he said, his father would never have dreamed of doing. Indeed, as loving as Alcott had been, in his own way, he had purportedly not touched Clive or Julia until they were fully two years old, claiming that he had been afraid he would drop or damage them somehow in the process. Privately, Henrietta thought this a very weak excuse, but she had kept her opinion to herself and put it down to the staid Victorianism in which Alcott had been raised.

Henrietta brushed Teddy's plump cheek with her finger as he continued to suck and then looked back at Edna, who had resumed her unpacking.

"How are things below stairs, Edna? Everything okay? Lording it over them?"

Edna laughed a little but kept her eyes on her work. "Well, I wouldn't say that, miss, but I do enjoy outranking nearly everyone, except Mrs. Caldwell and Mr. Billings, of course, though, I suppose, as head of the house back in London, I'm on the same level as Mrs. Caldwell? Oh, who knows!" she said, tossing a pair of undergarments onto the bed. "I was offered a private room next to Mrs. Caldwell's, which is saying a lot, really, but I said no, I was needed upstairs. I'll take the room next door, shall I? I don't mind bunking with the little mister," she said, nodding at Teddy.

"Pascal won't be bothered?"

"Nah. It's not for very long. And anyway, it'll be like old times, eh?"

Henrietta watched the young woman as she removed more items from the cases and reflected at how confident Edna was now compared to when she had first met her—in this very house. Edna had been just a timid junior maid then, and Henrietta a somewhat unwelcome guest, who had more of a tendency to help Edna with her chores than to sit with Antonia in the morning room drinking tea and gossiping about the goings-on at her club.

Once Henrietta and Clive were married, Antonia, perhaps noting the closeness of the two young women, had promoted Edna to be Henrietta's personal lady's maid—a wedding gift, she had said. Henrietta had initially protested, saying that she was not in need of a personal maid, but when she realized that as such, Edna's life would be much easier than it had been as a junior maid, she had reluctantly agreed. After their misadventures in Europe, however, Henrietta had seen fit to promote her once again—this time to head housekeeper, a position for which she, too, was much too young. But Henrietta didn't care; it was her house, and she delighted in the fact that she could do what she liked.

Both she and Clive had decided early on that they would try to operate their household with as few servants as possible, determined to do some of the work themselves, a vow that was proving a bit harder now that a lordship had been conferred upon Clive, which required, sadly, much more entertaining, not to mention travel. Up until now, however, they had managed in the London townhouse with only a shoestring staff, namely Edna, Pascal, a cook, and a chambermaid—Pascal at times doubling as a chauffeur and Edna as nanny. Edna seemed to truly love Teddy, and Pascal was proving to be as keen on luxury cars as Clive. And there were even times when the four of them sat down to play cards in the evening, a fact that would probably have caused poor Antonia, had she known, to faint.

"And how's Pascal getting on? Is Billings being kind?"

"Seems okay. Carter's a bit bent out of shape, seeing as he thinks *he's* Mr. Clive's valet. Wish I could tell the old bugger that Mr. Clive's never liked him, but that would be unkind, wouldn't it, miss?"

"A bit, yes."

Carter had been Alcott's valet since he—Alcott, that is— was just sixteen years old, and had traversed the ocean with him when the young gentleman had bravely sailed across to marry the fabulously rich young debutante Antonia Hewitt, a girl he had never even met. Since Alcott's untimely death, Carter had assumed he would begin assisting the young master of the house, though, technically, at thirty-eight, Clive wasn't exactly *young*, but Clive had refused to employ a valet. Until Pascal had come along, that is, but that had been a sort of accident and a much longer story.

Henrietta sat Teddy up on her lap and began rubbing his back in an attempt to burp him. He looked curiously around the darkened bedroom and smiled when he caught sight of Edna, who had begun playing peek-a-boo from behind one of Henrietta's skirts that she was in the process of folding.

"First Christmas for you!" She poked her head out from behind the skirt. "Wonder if Santa will come?" She popped out again, causing Teddy to gurgle with delight.

"Da da da da!" he cooed.

"Not 'Da-da,'" Edna said, tickling his wet chin. "Say 'Pa-pa!'"

Teddy gurgled again.

Henrietta gave him a little kiss on the head, breathing in the delicious smell of him. It still made her smile when she remembered the look of shock on Clive's face when she had first referred to him as "Papa," knowing as she did that he had assumed he would be addressed by Teddy and all subsequent children as "Father."

"Can you not be Papa until they are at least able to stand on two legs in short pants in front of you?" Henrietta had said with a little laugh and a kiss on Clive's cheek.

"Only if you are to be Mama," he had acquiesced with a smile.

Edna took Teddy. "Your Papa will be here in a moment. Which is why Mama needs to dress." She shifted Teddy onto her hip. "I've laid out the burgundy in the dressing room, miss. Do you need help?"

"No, take him through, though, would you, Edna? I'll call you when I need buttoning. Or I'll ring for someone."

"Don't you dare!" Edna darted into the adjoining room, Teddy still on her hip, a tendril of Edna's hair gripped tightly in his little fist.

With a sigh, Henrietta rose. She was very tired, but she knew she had to get dressed for cocktails below. She wandered over to the Christmas tree, a miniature Scotch pine in the corner, decorated, she noticed ruefully, with all of the orna-ments she had made last year—her and Clive's first Christmas together. She fingered a tiny star she had cut out of paper. That seemed so long ago.

She let out a little groan at the memory of her gift to him, a wooden sign with *Howard Detective Agency* carved into it and painted in gold. How ridiculous! She was so innocent then. Those days were long gone, as was her idea for Clive to form a detective agency. They had much bigger responsibilities and cares now.

She heard Clive enter the room, but before she could turn, she felt his arms go around her from behind.

"What are you thinking about?" he asked gently, resting his chin between her neck and her shoulder. He must have already washed and changed, because the smell of his cologne was divine.

"Oh, I don't know. That it was nice of your mother to have a tree put up for us, since I was so insistent about it last year. She even kept the ornaments I made. We just need to make a new popcorn string."

"She can be kind when she wants to be."

Henrietta turned to him. "I know. It's just . . . I somehow feel like nothing's changed, that I'm just little Henrietta Von Harmon, still trying to impress your mother."

Clive laughed out loud. "Don't let her get to you. She adores you. Especially now that you've produced an heir. *And* that you're Lady Linley. She can't wait to show you off at the club."

Henrietta sighed deeply. "Not the club. I don't think I can bear it. And, also, you make me sound like a breeding mare. I *am* capable of more than that, you know."

"Oh, don't I?" Clive said with a grin and kissed her.

Henrietta responded in kind, wrapping her arms behind his neck and fingering his hair. He was utterly handsome in his black-tie tuxedo. He had a few more gray hairs along his temples than when she had first met him, but she still found him supremely attractive. "What do you want for Christmas?" she asked huskily, finally breaking their kiss.

"You," he said, kissing her cheek and then her neck and then her chest.

"Be serious!" she laughed.

"I *am* serious. There's not a single thing I want." He rested his forehead against hers.

Henrietta allowed herself a few moments to stare into his warm hazel eyes. "I recognize that naughty look, Inspector, but we don't have time." She pulled away, but a seductive smile was still on her lips. "Come along." She tugged his lapels. "Duty calls."

CHAPTER 2

"But we have a duty to the poor, do we not?" Antonia insisted from where she was situated on the antique horsehair sofa in the drawing room.

"Of course we do, Mother, but I think it should be more than handing out a few trifles at Christmas to ease a guilty conscience." Clive's tone was dry.

"Don't be impertinent with me, Clive! You're not too old to scold, you know." She sipped her sherry pensively. "And I, for one, do *not* have a guilty conscience," Antonia went on, "and the gifts we give out at the club aren't *trifles*. They're quite substantial, and we've heard from several credible sources that the gifts are very much appreciated."

"Of course we'd be happy to help, Antonia." Henrietta set her sherry on the small Chippendale table near her and folded her hands in her lap. She looked stunning, as usual, and tonight had donned the deep burgundy gown that she had been fitted for at the House of Lanvin when they were in Paris. "What would you like us to do?"

Antonia threw a triumphant glare at Clive and then looked back at Henrietta. "Why don't you come with me to the club tomorrow morning, dear? The Committee for Christmas Gifts for the Unfortunate Poor will be there, and I—"

Clive interrupted her with a loud laugh, which produced yet another glare.

"Oh, come now, Mother. *The Committee for Christmas Gifts for the Unfortunate Poor*? Who thought of that name? And isn't it a tad condescending?"

Antonia drew herself up. "It is a committee that has been in existence since the founding of the club, Clive, as you very well know. You're just choosing to be obtuse on purpose. Perhaps you and Sidney should retire to the study if you're going to behave like a rube." She looked over at Sidney, perhaps for reinforcement, but he remained unmoving in his leather hooded armchair, his legs crossed and his fingers steepled under his nose.

"Now, Mother, I'm only teasing." Clive leaned against the fireplace mantel. "Go on. I do beg your pardon."

"As I was saying, the gifts have already been purchased weeks ago," Antonia said with a small sniff, "and tomorrow is the wrapping of them. And there's the final meeting of the Christmas Ball committee, of which I am head this year," she said with a little flourish.

Clive fought the urge to roll his eyes. He had forgotten how irritating his mother's climb up the social ladder was, all the more tiresome because she was already *at* the top, having married Alcott Howard, brother to the then Lord Linley. It had been *the* Chicago wedding of that generation, rivaled only perhaps by that of her now best friend, Victoria Braithewaite, who had married the second cousin of Woodrow Wilson. Clive wondered, however, if marrying Sidney Bennett, a mere lawyer, may have brought her down a rung or two, hence the need to rescramble toward the top.

"The committee would very much welcome your presence and advice, Henrietta. And we have a special favor to ask."

Henrietta shifted in her chair. "Well, I was planning to go see my family tomorrow, Antonia. Did Clive not tell you that?" She glanced at him. "They're most anxious to meet Teddy . . ."

Antonia frowned.

"Is there something else I could do on a different day perhaps? Maybe help distribute the gifts?"

"Heavens, no! The stewards at the club do that. It would take much too much time for us to drive all over Winnetka. And embarrassing, too. For the poor, that is. It's much better that a delivery person of sorts hands them their gifts. Not *us*! No, that would never do."

Clive badly wanted to comment, but he held his tongue and instead took a long drink of his cognac, glancing at the mantel clock as he did so and wondering how long before they could reasonably extract themselves. Not only was he getting more and more irritated by the minute, but he desperately wanted to make love to Henrietta. Since having Teddy, she had blossomed in a way he hadn't expected. She had been wildly attractive when they first met, but now she was positively beautiful. He looked across at her, her thick auburn hair swept up and her long lashes lowered. She positively glowed.

"What *can* we do, then?" Henrietta asked, taking a small sip of her sherry. "What is the favor you were planning to ask?"

"Well," Antonia drawled, looking from one to the other, "we are hoping that you and Clive will agree to open the Christmas Ball. To have Lord and Lady Linley open the festivities will simply be magnificent!"

"And quite a feather in your cap, eh, Mother?" Clive raised an eyebrow.

"Honestly, Clive. If your father were here, you'd not dare to speak to me in this way."

"That isn't true, Mother," Clive said wryly. "I've always spoken to you this way. And you're not going to bully us into increasing your social standing at the club. I don't—"

"Of course we will, Antonia," Henrietta said kindly, shooting Clive a look. "Personally, I can't wait to attend the Christmas Ball."

Why was she so eagerly siding with every irritating suggestion his mother made? Hadn't they agreed? He felt irritable and out of sorts tonight, though he wasn't sure why. He was back home, Henrietta and Teddy were safe, all was apparently well. So why did he feel so . . . so restless and annoyed? Perhaps he was happier in London living his other life than he had previously realized . . .

"Thank you, my dear. I knew I could count on you to see sense. It will be the event of the year!"

"Will Julia be attending?" Clive extracted his pipe from his pocket. "When does she arrive, anyway? Thought they'd be here by now."

"The twenty-third. And no, she and Glenn will not attend; that's one reason they are coming in after the fact. It wouldn't be appropriate, and you know it, Clive."

"For a divorced woman to attend? I thought Glenn's millions more than made up for it. All they'd need to do is make a sizable donation to the club and all would be forgotten. Is that not so?"

He glanced at Henrietta, and seeing her creased brow, supposed he had crossed the line. But he couldn't help it. He hated all of this social scrabbling nonsense.

"It will be marvelous to see them!" Henrietta picked up her sherry again as if she needed reinforcement. "I can't wait to see how Randolph, Jr. and Howard have grown. And Teddy can meet his two cousins."

"Yes, they are much changed," Antonia sniffed. "You will hardly recognize them."

"For the better, I think," Sidney put in. "Glenn's been good for them."

"Well, it was kind of them to give up their Christmas at home to join us here; don't you think, Clive?" Henrietta took a sip.

"Mmmm." Clive rubbed his chin. "Yes, for sure. I wish we could have made the wedding." Henrietta had been six months pregnant at the time of Julia and Glenn's wedding, and the doctor had advised that a ship voyage to New York and then a train to Texas was completely out of the question. Henrietta had urged Clive to go without her, but he had steadfastly refused, especially given her previous miscarriage.

"Oh! You didn't miss much," Antonia declared. "I mean, it was very small. Just Sidney and me, and Glenn's parents and brothers. It was held in a small chapel on the property. 'Mission style' I think is what they call it. The whole place is that way. Not my taste at all, but Julia claims to 'adore' it. You know how she is. Overly enthusiastic. The house is immense, I will say that. But, honestly, it's in the middle of nowhere."

"Well, that's generally the point of a ranch," Clive muttered as he lit his pipe.

Antonia let out a sigh. "And speaking of houses, it still pains me that you gave up Castle Linley, Clive, to live in the London house. Why? It's really not appropriate for the lord to abandon the ancestral home."

"Mother, we've been through all of this before. The estate was bankrupt. Uncle Montague inherited a dying behemoth, and when he died, Wallace couldn't afford the death tax. Simple as that."

"He's right, Antonia. It made more financial sense," Sidney added, finally offering an opinion.

"And it's supremely better for it to be used as a school for girls rather than as a home for three entitled people and an army of servants." Clive puffed deeply, trying to get the tobacco going.

"Who are all out of a job now, I might point out," Antonia snipped.

"Who are mostly employed at the school," he retorted. "Happily, I'm told."

"But surely something could have been done? To keep it in the family, that is?" She looked inquiringly at Sidney.

"I think it a very good use of the property, my dear. Capital idea."

Clive cringed a little. It grated on him whenever Sidney used "my dear" in addressing his mother. It had been the very same term of endearment his father had used for her. And why was he bandying about the word "capital" now, as if he had himself gone to Cambridge instead of Harvard Law? Was he so eager to fill his father's shoes, not to mention his bed . . .

Clive cleared his throat and made a beeline for the sideboard, where the crystal bottle of cognac sat on a silver tray. Contrary to Henrietta's accusations that he was bothered by his mother's marriage to Sidney, he, in actuality, didn't mind. He loved his mother, and in a certain way, he loved Sidney, too, who had been like a second father to him. But somehow being a thousand miles away when they married had prevented it from sinking in entirely. Now that he was back, however, seeing them here together as a couple, it made it harder to accept than he had thought.

"It's near Austin, isn't it?" Henrietta asked pertly. She was trying to change the subject, he knew, something she was superbly good at. "Glenn's ranch? Perhaps we should visit sometime, Clive."

"Yes, perhaps in the spring." He removed the crystal stopper with a clink and poured some cognac into his glass.

"We might think about expanding in the South," Sidney said. "Might be a good opportunity. I've been speaking with Glenn about it."

"Have you?" Clive look a long drink. "Well, you'll have to speak to the board. It's nothing to do with me anymore." Clive had never wanted anything to do with his father's company, Linley Standard, and didn't now, either. He had tried, briefly, to take the reins of the London branch, but his duties in the House of Lords and the new school at Castle Linley had eventually proved to be too much, and he had had to relegate it.

"As you wish." Sidney gave a slight nod. "But there's another matter I thought I might discuss with you, Clive." He stood and meandered toward the sideboard as well. "I've had Formby out to look at the stables. I think we should tear them down. Modernize."

"Tear down the stables?" Clive felt an uncomfortable twist in his gut. "Why?"

Sidney's face was one of surprise. "We discussed this briefly in the past. Don't you remember?"

"I seem to remember discussing the staff apartments above."

"Well, yes," Sidney gestured widely. "But if we are to completely renovate them, it makes sense to tear it all down and start fresh. After all, the stables are really rather redundant, seeing as Alcott sold the last of the horses . . . what? Thirty years ago? And it makes for a poor garage for the autos."

"It still serves a purpose. I don't see why we need to tear it all down just to paint and refurbish the staff apartments!" Clive argued.

"Well, that's what I said. Why do we need to change anything at all?" Antonia chimed in. Clive rubbed his brow. He did not need his mother's involvement in this.

"Clive," Henrietta said gently. "I thought we agreed on the need to remodel Highbury. And now that we're so far away, it's wonderful that Sidney has taken up the task, don't you think? Someone has to do it, after all."

"It wouldn't be anything garish, if that's what you're worried about, old boy. Formby assures me he can build something that will perfectly blend with the original construction."

"Just like yourself, I suppose?" Clive snapped. "And stop calling me 'old boy.'"

"Clive!" Antonia gasped.

Sidney stared at Clive for several moments. "No, it's quite all right," Sidney said quietly. "I quite understand. Perhaps we should call it a night."

Henrietta stood and approached Clive, looping her arm through his. "Yes, I think we're all overtired. We'll say good night." She gave Antonia and Sidney a brief nod, but before she could guide him toward the stairs, Clive pulled his arm back, his desire for intimacy now gone.

"I'm not a child to be taken off to bed. I'll come up when I'm ready." Roughly, he grabbed his glass from the mantel and marched off in the direction of the billiard room. A part of him knew he was overreacting, and he already regretted what he had said to Henrietta. But he was angry, and was tired of playing the role of the supplicant.

The lights in the billiard room were dimmed, and the servants had a fire going in the massive stone fireplace, in the event, however unlikely, that anyone might have wanted a game of pool after dinner. Clive picked up the eight ball and rolled it violently toward a corner pocket. It missed, bounced, and rolled slowly back to him.

Clive rolled it again, this time with much less force, and let it drift. He looked around the room. How many evenings had he spent here with his father, one of the last being the night he had asked him for his advice about marrying Henrietta? His father, he remembered, had told him to follow his heart.

God, how he missed him! The fact that it was Christmas made it even worse, and it doubly pained him that his father had never gotten to see his latest grandson, the heir he had so desired. Clive had finally done the thing his father most wanted of him, and now he wasn't here to see it. He slumped into one of the chairs by the fire. It was too little, too late. And not for the first time, he felt like a failure, especially in the eyes of his father.

CHAPTER 3

"It's too little, too late, as far as I'm concerned," Antonia grumbled to Henrietta. "Though I am glad that you changed your mind about today. After all, you can see your family any time, can't you?"

The two of them were seated side by side in the back of the Rolls enroute to the Winnetka Country Club, Antonia's beloved "home away from home," as Clive and Henrietta liked to privately joke. "He thinks he can just waltz in and apologize this morning as if nothing happened. Well, poor Sidney was quite hurt, you know. He's practically known Clive since he was a baby, and for him to treat him that way. It's really just too much, Henrietta."

Henrietta let out a deep breath. As vexed as she was with Clive, too, it wouldn't do to fan Antonia's fire. It needed damping, if anything, which is precisely why she had suggested that she come with her to the club this morning instead of going to the city as planned. All because Clive had acted the recalcitrant schoolboy, upset that his mother had remarried! It was ridiculously irritating.

She had been asleep when he had finally stumbled into their bedroom in the wee hours of the morning, but he had since apologized profusely.

"Honestly, Clive, you were horribly rude," Henrietta had said from where she sat at her vanity, combing out her hair, which, technically was Edna's job, but Edna was busy with Teddy.

"I know that," Clive groaned, sitting up in bed, his head in his hands—a telltale sign that it was throbbing. "I'll apologize; don't worry."

"Yes, but now I'll have no choice but to go to the club with your mother so that she can show me off like a prized possession or a trophy. It's not fair," she said to his reflection in her vanity mirror as she put a final pin in her hair. "Ma was looking forward to seeing Teddy." Henrietta wasn't exactly sure this was true, but Elsie, she knew, was desperate to see him.

"I'll make it up to you."

"I've heard that one before. And don't think it will be between the sheets!"

Clive grinned roughly. "But I really will." He threw the covers off and wandered over to her. "I promise, darling." He kissed the top of her head. "I'll think of something very special."

"You mustn't mind him," Henrietta said, pulling her gaze from the festive Christmas market they were passing now in downtown Winnetka. Shoppers were strolling from booth to booth with large packages in their arms and pulling children behind them. "You know what he's like. His bark is worse than his bite."

"I suppose," Antonia grumbled. "But he has no idea how hard it's been for me since Alcott passed. And in case he thinks that Sidney is some sort of gold digger, he's not! I can assure him that Sidney is quite a wealthy man in his own right, serving Linley Standard all those years, never marrying. And . . ." She paused, as if deciding whether to proceed. ". . . The truth is that Sidney and I were in love once upon a time, *before* I married Alcott. But there was nothing we could do."

Henrietta bit her lip. She had already heard part of this tale from Clive but quickly decided to pretend she hadn't. "You were?" she asked innocently.

"Yes. My father was insistent that I marry into the aristocracy," Antonia went on, "and that was that." She tugged at her gloves. "But that is a story for another time," she muttered, a decision Henrietta thought wise, as she knew from her own experiences with Fritz that he was probably listening to every word.

They pulled into the long drive of the club, lined on both sides with rose bushes, which were sadly dormant now in the frigid December air. Fritz stopped under the portico, and Henrietta glanced at Antonia, whose eyes, she noted, held more than a flicker of eagerness, as if she were a general about to enter the fray with a new secret weapon.

Fritz exited the car as quickly as his old body could manage and came around to open the doors, first for Antonia and then Henrietta.

"We'll be a few hours, Fritz," Antonia called as she eagerly bustled toward the grand glass double doors.

"Very good, madam."

Henrietta followed, taking in a few extra deep breaths. She knew what was expected of her today, and she had decided on the drive over to play it up. After all, she had been acting most of her life—starting all the way back when she worked as a twenty-six girl for Mr. Hennessey at his corner tap, Poor Pete's, at thirteen. She had had to pretend she was much older than she actually was, enduring men's hands sliding across her bottom, laughing at their jokes in hopes of bigger tips. Taking on the role of Lady Linley for a bunch of elderly old gossips would be easy in comparison, perhaps even a little fun. She should have been an actress, she thought, as she stepped through into the main foyer of the club.

It had been a couple of years since she had been here for her wedding reception, but a flood of memories now resurrected. Clive had surprised her by hiring the famous Helen Forrest to sing. It was a day of extreme luxury and elegance such as she had never even imagined, a perfect fairy-tale wedding, and yet, now that she was Lady Linley and had been invited to any number of palaces and castles in Europe, the little Winnetka Country Club now paled in comparison, a fact that made her not a little sad.

A steward stepped forward to take their coats.

"Thank you, Noland," Antonia said, as the young man removed her fur coat for her. "Is Mrs. Braithewaite here yet?"

"Yes, madam." His address was perfectly correct, but Henrietta detected a slight flippancy in his tone of which she did not approve. The young man handed Antonia's coat to an even younger assistant, who looked to be no more than fifteen or sixteen, and then moved to take Henrietta's things, but not before letting his eyes roam to her shapely legs. The cheek! She took a step back and slid out of her mink herself, handing it to him with a stern raised eyebrow.

"Mrs. Braithewaite is in the Chesapeake room, ladies." He gave a mock bow.

"I swear they get younger every year," Antonia muttered to Henrietta as she hurried deeper into the club. "I blame the war. It's impossible to get good help these days."

Henrietta, though she had been in the same class as "the help" not so very long ago, tended now, from her current vantage point of privilege, to agree. She followed Antonia through the front "gathering room," as it was called, noting how lovely it looked all decorated for Christmas. Evergreen roping, interspersed with candles and pinecones, ran along the large stone fireplace on the west wall, and in the far corner was the tallest Christmas tree Henrietta thought she had ever seen. It was bedecked with red and gold ornaments placed in perfect symmetry and with gold ribbons that twisted vertically from the top of the tree all the way down, as if they were rays of the shimmering gold star at the peak. And on each of the side tables perched amongst the dark leather sofas and armchairs grouped around the room were more candles trimmed with tiny clusters of holly and bright-red berries. It was lovely to look at, and where Henrietta would have once been eager for her younger siblings to see it, now, of course, she thought of Teddy.

Antonia, however, seemed immune to the festive décor around her and rushed straight through the elegant room to get to the Chesapeake room, a smaller chamber beyond.

Victoria Braithewaite emerged from within just as Antonia and Henrietta arrived at the paneled wooden doors, which were slightly ajar.

"Here you are!" Victoria exclaimed. "We'd quite given you up, Antonia." She gave the air nearest Antonia's right cheek a kiss. "And Henrietta," she said with what looked like a forced smile. "My, how you've filled out," she said, looking her up and down. "Motherhood suits you, I suppose."

Henrietta gritted her teeth. "Hello, Mrs. Braithewaite," she said in mock sweetness. "How lovely to see you. You've filled out, too." She batted her eyes innocently.

Victoria's twisted smile twisted more. "It's so nice of you to join us. I'm sure you have so many other appointments. Seeing friends and family and whatnot. They're in the city, aren't they?" She said the word *city* as if she were tasting an unsavory morsel. "Somewhere near the Schwinn factory?"

"Well, I wouldn't say that, would you, Henrietta? It's more Palmer Square. Not far from Potter Palmer's mansion." Antonia gave her head a little tilt. "Isn't that right, Henrietta?"

"Yes. Very near." Henrietta had no desire to get involved in Antonia and Victoria Braithewaite's rivalry, but she couldn't, in good conscience, abandon Antonia to this she-wolf.

"It's a shame you're not here for longer. Antonia positively pines for Clive."

Antonia let out a strangled little chuckle. "Oh, but I *completely* understand. They are *so* very busy. Clive's duties in the House of Lords keep him eternally employed. Why, just last week, did he not meet with the Duke of Devonshire?" Antonia asked Henrietta sweetly. "And Henrietta, here, had the Duchess of Kent for tea, is that not so? She's in *such* demand."

"Yes, so nice of you to accommodate everyone in that small London townhouse. Shame Clive let the castle go. But, well," Victoria said with a feigned sigh, "these are the times we live in, aren't they? Seems everyone has it hard. Well," she paused to give a little laugh, "everyone except Hugh, of course. He claims to have had an exceptional year last year, but what would I know about that? And, anyway, it's positively gauche to discuss finance, isn't it?" She chuckled again. "And, at Christmas! Speaking of, I suppose I should get back to work wrapping these gifts."

She stepped aside and pushed the door open wider to reveal a massive walnut table, normally reserved perhaps for private board meetings, but which was now covered with boxes and sheets of wrapping paper and ribbons, and behind which stood two young women, rather haphazardly engaged in the wrapping of said boxes. Henrietta recognized the plumper girl to be Victoria's daughter, Beatrice, but she did not know the other one.

Antonia, apparently still reeling from Victoria's snipes, no doubt sensed a chance to one-up her "friend," and stepped forward eagerly. "Charlotte," Antonia said grandly to the other girl, "you must allow me to introduce my daughter-in-law, *Lady Linley*." She said it slowly and deliberately. "Miss Charlotte MacKenzie, Lady Linley. Lady Linley, Miss Charlotte MacKenzie. Charlotte is staying with the Braithewaites for Christmas, isn't that so?"

"Yes." Victoria, frowning now, drew herself up. "Charlotte is the daughter of one my very best friends in New York, Phillipa MacKenzie née Astor," she said with relish.

"Pleased to meet you," Henrietta said to Charlotte with a smile. "Hello, Beatrice," she added, addressing the quiet girl currently struggling with some ribbon.

Beatrice looked up briefly from the ribbon she was attempting to tie. "Hello, Henrietta," she said without expression and then resumed her work.

Henrietta had, of course, met Beatrice Braithewaite at several club events, but she had in truth spoken to her little. She was a shy young woman who seemed to have little to say, especially in the shadow of her formidable mother. She wore her dull-brown hair pulled tightly back, and it was difficult to see the color of her eyes through her thick eyeglasses. At twenty-nine, she was considered a confirmed spinster, though

Victoria, Henrietta knew—thanks to Antonia's gossip—still had high hopes of marrying her off, though maybe not to someone so esteemed as she had once hoped, say when Beatrice was a mere seventeen.

"At this point, she'd be lucky to fob poor Beatrice off on a banker," Antonia had twittered more than once over tea. "I mean, Beatrice is a very nice girl, but I do think Victoria was being a bit unrealistic. There was a time when she was convinced that *Alfred Vanderbilt* was to make an offer, but, alas, no. Well, I could have told her that, but Victoria does have her own ideas. And then, after that, there was the trip to Europe to try to arrange something with some Italian nobleman. Or maybe he was Swiss. One never knows with foreigners. It's impossible to keep them straight. Count Renalo, I think his name was. But that, too, failed. Apparently, Count Renalo was more than willing, but it was Beatrice herself that refused in the end. Didn't know she had it in her. I mean, she barely speaks above a whisper. Victoria, of course, was furious."

"Pleased to meet you," Charlotte said charmingly as she waved about the scissors she was holding. "Do you have an accent? Oh, please say that you do!"

Henrietta smiled. "I'm afraid not. Neither my husband nor I are British."

"Really? How odd! I mean, being a lord and lady, that is."

"It *is* odd." Victoria sniffed. "I'm sure they'll find it was some mistake in the will. I've tried to tell her," Victoria said to Henrietta with a nod at Antonia, "but she insists she's right. Well, you know what they say, 'Pride goeth before a fall.'"

"It isn't a matter of *a will*," Antonia said primly, keeping her voice even. "It is the English law of progeniture. My husband's brother held the seat until he passed last year," she said in Charlotte's direction, "and the title then went to my son, Clive. There really is no question."

"But wasn't there a son? Two sons, I believe," Victoria insisted.

"Yes, Lord Linley *did* have two sons." There was a trace of exasperation in Antonia's voice now. "One died on the Somme and the other was proved to be . . . illegitimate." Antonia patted her hair.

"Happens in the best of families, doesn't it?" Victoria simpered, as if she were a cat that caught the canary.

"Yes, well, as it turned out, the title went to Clive," Antonia said to Charlotte.

"How extraordinary!" Charlotte exclaimed. "To find yourself suddenly an aristocrat! What's the king like?" She turned her attention to Henrietta. "Have you met him? Or the queen?"

Henrietta bit her lips at the thought of how she spent most of her days in a committee meeting in some dreary church hall politely sipping weak tea, or else, if she *did* have a moment at home, it was spent on the floor playing with Teddy.

"I haven't, but Clive has. He and some of the other peers are to travel to Edinburgh after the holidays to have a confluence of sorts with His Royal Highness."

"Oh, you're sure to go, too, aren't you?" Antonia almost begged. "Think of the opportunity! To . . . to see the countryside, I mean." Her eyes flashed.

"Very probably, yes. It depends on whether the queen attends. If so, wives will be invited. Otherwise, it will probably be lords only." Henrietta looked at each of the ladies, who were rapt with attention, even Victoria Braithewaite, which was a coup for Antonia, in and of itself.

"And speaking of sons, how is poor Dennis?" Antonia asked with false sincerity.

Privately, Henrietta thought it rude that Antonia would refer to the young man as "poor" simply because he had been born with a twisted foot.

"Oh, he's marvelous!" Victoria gushed. "He's just finishing up his degree, and then he's off to Yale to begin medical school."

"It's wonderful that he can get around so well. I—"

"What are you wrapping?" Henrietta interrupted, deciding it was time to turn the conversation. She nodded at the array of items on the table.

"We're wrapping gifts for the 'unfortunate poor,'" Beatrice murmured, her eyes shifting nervously to her mother as if for approval.

"I see," Henrietta said politely, trying to ignore Beatrice's labeling of the poor as *unfortunate*, though, she supposed, they were. "What are you giving them? I assume by the look of it that the contents of each box will be the same?"

"Yes," Charlotte answered before Beatrice had a chance. "Each family will get a box containing a Bible, a fountain pen, a scarf, a bag of walnuts, a small box of chocolates, a bag of marbles, and a set of jacks," she said, pointing to each item as she named them. "The marbles and the jacks are for the children, obviously."

"What if a family doesn't have children?" Henrietta asked.

"Not have children?" Victoria interjected. "Of course they have children. All the poor have scads of children. That's one reason they're poor!"

Coming from a family of eight children, Henrietta resented this comment, but she kept it to herself. "I see."

"The pen is for the father," Charlotte went on eagerly, "the scarf for the mother, and the walnuts, the chocolates, and the Bible are for them all to share, obviously."

Henrietta cleared her throat. "Yes, these are lovely gifts, but I'm wondering though," she said tentatively, "if a couple of blankets, a tin of smoked ham, a block of cheese, some bread, and maybe a tin of coffee might be more appreciated."

Victoria's brow furrowed. "But this is what we *always* give them. The committee has discussed it in detail for months."

"Yes, well, just an idea." She smiled politely. "Maybe for next year."

"My, someone likes to be in charge, doesn't she?" Victoria muttered, making a show of tidying a pile of loose tissue paper. "Not back in the country two minutes, and she's already telling us our business." Victoria puffed up her very full chest.

"Mother," Beatrice chastised, her face pink. "Henrietta is just trying to help. We could use some new ideas sometimes."

"I think you meant to say *Lady Linley*," Antonia corrected sweetly.

"*Henrietta* is just fine," Henrietta said, daring to shoot a little glare at Antonia. She pulled out a chair. "Here, give me a box. I'll help wrap."

"But, Henrietta, we're meant to meet with the Christmas Ball committee now to discuss any last-minute details, and, as the *head*,"—she put a hand to her chest—"I really shouldn't be late." She nodded in the direction of the grand ballroom at the back of the club.

"Yes, so kind of you to take on that onerous task," Victoria purred. "Seeing as no one else wanted it. I—"

"Why don't you go ahead, Antonia," Henrietta interrupted, "and I'll join you soon. I don't think I'll be of much real use in the meeting, as I'm *sure* you have all of the final details in hand. I'd be more productive here if I help Beatrice and Charlotte, don't you think?" She eyed the woefully tall stack of unwrapped boxes.

Antonia stood, bristling.

"Yes, how kind of you, dear," she said finally, forcing a smile. "Victoria's call for volunteers for her committee fell rather short, didn't it, dear? Such a shame." She tsked and then, with one more look around the room, regally exited.

Henrietta reached for a sheet of wrapping paper, knowing full well she would get an earful on the way home. "So, ladies, I suggest we get started!"

CHAPTER 4

"We should get started," Elsie said to Anna, Doris, and Donny, all of whom were assembled around her at the thick wooden kitchen block. It had taken some urging, but Elsie had managed to commandeer the kitchen away from the cook—or *Chef,* as he insisted on being called—for the afternoon. "We need to get these Christmas cookies ready by the time the boys arrive home tonight."

"You won't let Grandfather send *me* away, will you, Elsie?" Donny whined.

"No, of course not."

"Then why did you let him send the big boys?"

"Well, that was a long time ago, and Grandfather has changed. In fact, he said the boys can choose to stay here next term if they want. Or they can return to boarding school. It's up to them now."

"Really?" Donny's eyes widened. "But where would they sleep? In my room?"

Elsie laughed. "There's plenty of room in this big house. We all fit before, didn't we?" It amazed Elsie that her youngest siblings seemed to have no memory of their ratty apartment on Armitage where all nine of them had crammed into four small rooms before currently falling on these better times. "Anna," she said gently to the littlest child. "Why don't you open the cocoa powder for me? That's it."

"What do *I* get to do?" Doris pouted.

"You go get the rolling pin. Donny," she preempted before he could likewise complain, "you go get the cookie cutters. They're there." She pointed. "The bottom drawer. Yes, that's it."

One of the things that had become evident since she and Gunther and Anna had come back to live in the old Palmer Square house was how Doris and Donny had begun to mature a bit. Previously, the twins had still been quite babyish, though they were already five years old. Now, with the introduction of Anna into their lives as a sort of little sister, they seemed to have grown up a bit, though, in actuality Anna was really their niece, Elsie mused. It was obviously too complicated of a relationship for the children to understand, but from the very first day Anna had arrived, Doris and Donny had nonetheless enjoyed showing the shy, nearly silent little girl all around the house, the gardens, and the immense park just outside their front door. And it was good for Anna, too. She was finally coming out of her shell a bit.

Elsie scooped some flour into the sifter and squeezed the handle, raining down a faint shower of flour onto the chopping block. "See?" she said to Anna. "You do it now."

"Can I?" Donny asked.

"In a minute. Look, now we have a nice little layer of flour so that the dough doesn't stick." She reached into the mixing bowl, scooped out a ball of sticky dough, and plopped it onto the bed of flour. Now we put a little flour on the roller," she explained, dusting it with her fingers. "And now we roll."

"Let me, Elsie!" Donny cried.

"No, Donny. I'm going to do the first batch because the dough is hardest to work with right now because it's fresh. It'll toughen up as we go along and then maybe." She looked at Anna, who was watching keenly. Elsie steadily rolled the dough until it was roughly in the shape of a thin circle.

"There we are." Elsie set down the roller. "Now the fun part. Here, each of you take a cookie cutter. That's it. Choose the one you like best." She waited for them to choose and then herself took a star from the ones that were left. "Now you press it down, like so," she demonstrated, carefully pressing and then lifting the cutter to reveal a perfect star shape. "You try now."

Doris and Donny immediately thrust their cutters onto the dough, but Anna merely watched, a cookie cutter in the shape of a stocking clenched in her hand.

"Here, Anna, like this." Elsie guided her little fingers and helped her press the cutter into the soft dough. At the sight of the stocking outline left behind, Anna smiled.

"Now what?" Doris asked.

"Now we put them carefully on the pan." With a spatula, Elsie began sliding the shapes onto a cookie sheet. "And then, the really fun part!" She reached for the bowls of nuts, cocoa shavings, coconut flakes, colored sugar, nonpareils, and jimmies she had prepared earlier.

"Oooh! Can we have some?" Donny begged.

"You can each have one nut, but we have to save the rest for the cookies!"

Doris and Donny's chubby fingers reached for the nuts, but Anna held back, a finger in her mouth, a habit Elsie was trying to break her of.

"Do you want a nut?" she asked, gently tapping the girl's finger away. Anna shook her head. Elsie continued to lift the cookies onto the pan and then took a pinch of colored sugar and sprinkled it onto a bell. "See? We have to make them very pretty for our Christmas party!"

As the children eagerly began sprinkling the cookies with toppings, Elsie gathered up the dough scraps, formed them loosely into a ball, and began to roll again. She was excited for Christmas especially because it meant they would all be together! It had been months since she had seen her brothers before they left for boarding school out East. Herbie had written faithfully, but the other two, of course, had not. Thankfully, Herbie's letters usually included *some* news of Eddie and Jimmy, otherwise, she would know nothing of how either of them were doing. She longed to see the three of them, but she was particularly anxious to see Jimmy. She had been so worried about him. He was a mere seven when Grandfather had sent them away, and she couldn't wait to give him the cuddles she once had.

Only Eugene would be absent for Christmas, seeing as he was now a Private First Class in the army and stationed at Fort Monroe in Virginia and couldn't get away, or said he couldn't, anyway. Elsie hated to admit it, but as much as she wanted the family to be gathered under one roof, she was secretly relieved when he had written to say that he wouldn't be making it home for Christmas. He had come home last year, and though she had been impressed at the time by how much he had grown up, he had proven that he could still be abrasive and temperamental. And he didn't always get along with Clive. Which was another of her worries.

While it was true that Clive had been here for Christmas last year, Elsie had been so consumed by her own woes at the time that she had barely given Clive two thoughts. Though Ma was theoretically still the head of the house, she rarely came out of her room now, which essentially left the managing of the Palmer Square house and thus the hosting of Christmas to Elsie—and Gunther, of course, though he was of little real help when it came to all of the Christmas preparations. Consequently, she fretted about what Clive might think of their little party. She knew this was ungenerous—he had never once said an unkind word to her—but she couldn't help it. Who knew what he was used to for Christmas dinner at Highbury, not to mention his *castle* in England? She groaned, and her stomach positively clenched at the thought of how much shopping there was left to do!

She reached for a cookie cutter and hurriedly pressed it over and over around the dough, but when she tried to lift the raw cookies with the spatula, they buckled—she had rolled the dough too thin. With a sigh, she scraped it all back into a ball and started over. She hoped Ma would not act up during the party. Elsie began rolling the dough again, this time not pressing so hard, and wished that Ma's nurse, Miss Flanagan, could stay and assist her during the party, but Elsie knew it was unfair to keep Miss Flanagan from her own family—an aunt and a cousin, she had mentioned, who lived in Bridgeport—on Christmas Eve.

Ma had become increasingly ornery and forgetful these last few months. Henrietta would hardly know her, Elsie predicted, or . . . worse . . . would Ma know Henrietta? Oftentimes, when Elsie came into the room, Ma would ask her who she was, or else would call Elsie "Mother," which was unsettling in the extreme. Elsie had tried to write to Henrietta about it, but Henrietta never addressed it in her letters back.

Elsie cut the dough again, and this time it worked better. She quickly added more cookies to the pans for the children to continue decorating, though it seemed that there was already more sugar on the floor than on the cookies. But even if Ma did behave, she mused, there were still the Hennesseys to worry about. They were constantly asking after Henrietta, whom they still called "their girl," which was odd, considering that they had three (or, rather, two now, as Billy had died in the war) children of their own. They were sadly, though, somewhat estranged from their children, which was why, perhaps, Elsie reasoned, they seemed so attached to Henrietta. Elsie was beginning to regret asking them to Christmas, but then again, it had barely been her decision, as the Hennesseys had practically invited themselves!

"Won't be any trouble for us to stop over, will it, William? None a'tall!" Mrs. Hennessey had declared upon "accidentally" running into a very surprised Elsie as she was strolling in Palmer Square Park with the children not but a few weeks ago—surprised because the Hennesseys lived nowhere near Palmer Square.

"What are you doing here?" Elsie had queried, keeping one eye on Doris and Donny and Anna, who were now engaged in a game of tag. "I mean, it's lovely to see you, but . . . why, it's so far for you!"

"Far? Ain't far. And anyways, we came in hopes of running into *you*. If you weren't here, we was gonna ring the bell, weren't we, William? Come to see how yer gettin' on. Any news of Henrietta? She don't write all that often, but I suppose havin' a little 'un keeps her busy. Still can't believe our girl has a baby! Don't seem right, does it, William? But then again, she *is* a married woman now. We must remember that. But why she has to live in England is beyond me. When's she coming home next, Elsie?"

"Er . . . Christmas," Elsie faltered, shielding her eyes from the weak late-autumn sun.

"Christmas? Why, we'll be sure to come over. Won't be any trouble, will it, William? Don't have any Christmas plans at all! Don't worry; we don't expect anything fancy. A roast turkey and all the trimmings will do us. We'll bring a bottle of wine, won't we, William? When you having it, Elsie? Christmas Eve or Christmas Day?"

"Well . . . Christmas Eve," Elsie mumbled, her panic rising.

"Splendid! What time?"

"Six?"

"That'll do us! Well, we best get goin'. Nice seein' ya, Elsie. Tell Henrietta we was askin' after her!" Mrs. Hennessey called over her shoulder as she and Mr. Hennessey began walking back across the park. Elsie felt a little bit nauseous watching them go and wondering what had just happened.

It seemed absurd that the Hennesseys were now also coming to Christmas, but how could she say no to the people who had practically raised Henrietta after she had begun scrubbing floors at Poor Pete's just after her thirteenth birthday when Pa had . . . well, had died? And, indeed, when Clive wished to ask for Henrietta's hand in marriage, it was Mr. Hennessey to whom he had gone, hat in hand and in all sincerity.

Gunther, she knew, would not mind having them—as a professor at Loyola, he enjoyed having interesting and varied guests around their dinner table and was therefore always asking people to come dine with them. But would one call the Hennesseys interesting? Certainly varied. She just hoped that Henrietta and Clive wouldn't mind . . .

"Elsie! Come see what Anna's found!"

Elsie shook herself from her jumbled thoughts and saw that both Donny and Anna had already bored of the cookie decorating project and had wandered over to the back door. Doris turned from where she was still faithfully applying a rather large number of nonpareils on one thin blob of dough (this one would be a crunchy one!) and ran to see what Donny and Anna were looking at.

Elsie set her rolling pin down and wiped her hands on her apron and slowly made her way over to where the children were crouched. "What is it?"

Doris and Donny moved aside to reveal Anna standing proudly with a large tabby cat in her arms. "Anna found it outside the door!" Donny cried.

"What's this?" Elsie asked, her hands on her hips.

Anna held the cat higher.

"Use words," Elsie instructed gently.

"Kitty." The girl's voice was high and tiny, like an enchanted fairy.

"You've found a kitty, have you?" Elsie smiled. She herself had a proclivity for collecting strays, Gunther and Anna included. She scratched the cat's head and ears and then felt a collar. Oh! This was not a stray cat at all, but a lost cat! "Here," she said, taking it from Anna. "Let me see." She examined the collar, but it did not have a tag.

"Can we keep her?" Donny exclaimed. "What should we name her? How about Merry. For Merry Christmas?"

Elsie placed the cat back into Anna's arms. "No, we can't keep her, Donny. She belongs to someone else."

"No, she don't!"

"Doesn't. She *does* belong to someone else because she has a collar. See?" Elsie fingered it. "She's probably just lost. Her owner will be looking for her."

"Oh, but please, Elsie! You never let us do anything!" Doris cried.

"That isn't true, you spoiled girl. And how would you feel if we had a cat and someone kept him? Wouldn't we be sad? Perhaps there is another little boy or girl," she glanced at Anna, "who is crying in her bed this very moment because her poor kitty is gone."

Anna looked down at the cat, her bottom lip quivering a bit.

"Tell you what," Elsie intervened before tears broke out. "Let's give her some scraps and some milk, and then you can bundle up and take her round to the neighbors. See if anyone is missing a cat. Won't that be fun? You'll be like Santa delivering a special gift."

"Oh, yes!" cried Doris and Donny. "What should we feed her?" They ran toward the larder. Elsie followed. *This was just what she needed!* She didn't have time to fool with a missing cat, and yet she couldn't just throw it out into the cold.

While Doris and Donny rummaged through the larder, Elsie opened the icebox and removed a bottle of milk. "Get a dish," she called to the twins, "and we'll pour some milk." She hesitated to give the cat any of the roast chicken that had been stored there by Chef. Perhaps bread would be better. "Doris, open the breadbox and see if there are any scraps of bread."

Donny came running up with a bowl, and Elsie gently poured the milk. "Maybe I should carry it—"

"Oh, no!" cried Doris, who had already secured a crust of bread and had run to the back door.

"What is it?" Elsie did not look up but kept her eyes trained on the too-full bowl of milk she had taken from Donny and was attempting to carry.

"Anna and the kitty are gone!"

CHAPTER 5

"What do you mean they're gone?" Antonia snipped into the telephone receiver she was holding with both hands, her voice unusually high. "Have you telephoned the police? I see. Well, yes. I see. Very good. I'll ring you back." Antonia set down the receiver with a bang and turned to face Henrietta and Clive, who were the only other two in the morning room, save Billings, of course, who was standing at attention in his usual perch in the corner.

"Is everything all right, Antonia?" Henrietta asked from where she still sat at the table, trying to decide if she felt up to tackling the grapefruit in front of her. "I couldn't help but hear you mention the police."

"Seems there's been a theft at the club!" Antonia uncharacteristically twisted her hands for a brief few moments before she forced them apart, her eyes meanwhile darting toward Clive, who was hidden behind an open newspaper.

"A theft! Of what?" Henrietta wondered what could possibly have been carried off. The silver? The china? Perhaps there was a safe with cash? She plucked the cherry from atop the sliced grapefruit half and plopped it into her mouth.

"The Christmas gifts!" Antonia responded, though she did not look at Henrietta and instead continued to stare at Clive, whose only reaction was to slowly turn a page of the newspaper.

"The Christmas gifts? Why would anyone steal *them*?" Henrietta asked, also throwing Clive a look, which likewise bounced off the paper just as Antonia's had done. "Are you sure they weren't just misplaced? Maybe the stewards moved them?"

"That was Victoria on the phone, and she's *quite* sure. She's had the staff turn the whole place upside down. They're nowhere to be found! And if they're not found soon, we'll be forced to get the police involved, which will not reflect well on the club. Can you imagine? Police cars? Sirens? Lights flashing?"

"If you are attempting to goad me into action, it won't work," Clive said from behind the paper.

"But, Clive, you *must* help us! Wasn't this what you were always going on about? Wanting to be a detective? I mean, thank goodness that's all over and done with now, a phase I put it down to, but for once you might use your skills for something *worthwhile*."

Henrietta winced, knowing that this was probably not the right thing to say to spur Clive on. As predicted, he lowered the paper and glared at his mother now. "Finding Father's killer wasn't worthwhile?"

"Yes, well, besides that. Oh, Clive! Must you be so disagreeable?"

Clive folded the paper and tossed it on the table. "Mother, this hardly requires my attention. I'm sure the police will handle it. And you needn't worry about drawing negative attention to the club; they're hardly going to race over, sirens blaring, for something this trivial. They'll assign it to some sod who will turn up in plain clothes—very discreet, you can be assured—to ask questions. If you're lucky, it'll be Lieutenant Davis. If you're unlucky, it'll be the chief."

At the mention of Lieutenant Davis, Henrietta brightened. She would like to see him again, to see how he was faring after the "accident" in which the three of them had been involved. There was something about him that intrigued her.

"I'm not going to argue with you, Clive," Antonia snipped. "That's just what you want. And it isn't trivial! Those gifts cost the committee over five hundred dollars to put together. That's a lot of money, and we don't have time to go out and rebuy everything, especially this close to Christmas. Everything will be picked over, for one thing," she mused, as if actually considering the possibility for a moment.

"Why don't you just give the poor some cash?" Clive asked, leaning back and casually crossing his legs. "They'd probably rather have that than a Bible and some nuts anyway."

"Don't be cheeky, Clive. It doesn't suit. And even if we wanted to do that, there's no time to take up yet another collection."

"Why don't *you* front it?" He looked around the lavish morning room and grinned. "Sell another one of Father's paintings. Or better yet, *I'll* front it. There, problem solved."

"But that isn't the point, Clive, and you know it! These gifts are supposed to be from the committee, from the club! And think of the children. For many of them, this is the only gift they'll receive." Her tone was one of near defeat now.

"Clive, perhaps we could have a look around," Henrietta said gently. "It can't hurt. The whole thing is a bit odd, don't you think? I mean, who would do such a thing?"

"It has the feel of a prank to me." Clive said dismissively.

Henrietta stood up and came around to his side of the table and tousled his hair. "Where's your Christmas spirit, Scrooge? Let's help your mother, shall we?"

Clive gazed up at her and held her eyes. "Seems I'm out-numbered," he said, breaking into a small smile and looking at her with that wistful way of his. He let out a little sigh. "Billings, have Fritz bring my Alfa around. I feel like driving."

"Very good, m'lord."

"And stop calling me 'm'lord.'"

"Yes, m'lord."

"You don't always have to agree with my mother, you know." Clive said, shifting the Alfa Romeo into a higher gear as they sped down Sheridan Road.

Henrietta laughed. "I did this for you, Inspector. I know you're bored to tears sitting around doing nothing, and this is right up your alley. Consider this your Christmas gift from me."

"You don't fool me for a minute, you know." He shot her a quick sideways glance. "It's *you* who wants to investigate."

"All right, fine. I'll claim it, since you always have to win."

"I haven't the foggiest idea of what you're talking about, darling," he said nonchalantly as he pulled into the Winnetka Country Club property. He drove slowly down the long lane and stopped adroitly under the green-and-white-striped awning. A valet hurried to open the door for him, and Clive tossed him the keys as he climbed out. "Don't scratch it."

Another valet opened the door for Henrietta, and she gracefully exited, pulling her fur around her tighter. She had donned her mink, knowing it would please Antonia for her to show up in style, especially after she had previously disappointed her by stooping to something so lowly as to help the gift-wrapping committee. She and Clive had offered to bring her along with them in the Alfa, but she had declined, saying she would follow with Sidney and that, anyway, the Alfa was a deathtrap.

Clive and Henrietta entered the gathering room, where several people were nervously milling about, talking together in hushed voices. Henrietta spotted Victoria Braithewaite sagged in an armchair, limply fanning herself, despite the frigid air outside, with a spare Winnetka Country Club Christmas card. She looked to be perspiring. Beatrice sat nearby.

"Oh! Clive. Your mother said you were on the way," Victoria exclaimed, struggling to stand. Beatrice immediately stood and gripped her mother's arm to help her. "This whole affair is simply unconscionable!" Mrs. Braithewaite moaned. "What fiend would steal Christmas gifts from the poor!"

"Maybe whoever did it didn't realize they were *for* the poor, Mother." Beatrice offered quietly. "Or maybe they were poor themselves. Or maybe they had some other reason."

Victoria shot her a look of rebuke. "I don't understand you, Beatrice. Whatever the reason, it was a shameful thing to do! Steal presents at Christmas? Have they no fear of God?"

Clive rubbed his brow. "Look. Let's start at the beginning, shall we? How many gifts are we talking about?" He looked at Henrietta.

Henrietta blinked, trying to guess. "Maybe fifty?"

"Fifty-six," Beatrice put in shyly.

Clive let out a low whistle. "Not a quick job then. Where were they kept?"

"In the storage room." Victoria waved absently to her left. "Was it locked?"

"I should think so!" Victoria looked at Beatrice for confirmation. "Well? Was it?"

"I believe so," the girl answered meekly. "Do you remember, Henrietta?"

"Yes, I think I remember seeing the steward lock it. But I wasn't really paying much attention, to be honest."

"I'll need to talk to this steward," Clive said. "What's his name?"

"It's Noland, I believe," Beatrice answered.

"Surname?" Clive asked.

"I'm not sure. Peters, I think." Beatrice's shoulders briefly raised and lowered.

"For goodness' sake, Beatrice, do *not* shrug!" Victoria scolded. "It is horribly unladylike, not to mention altogether too modern. That's all the youth, especially the young men, do these days is shrug. It's no better than apes! And what is it supposed to mean, anyway? Disapproval? Bewilderment? Confusion?"

Beatrice pressed her lips together, a faint blush spreading across her freckled nose and cheeks.

"And stand up straight!"

Beatrice immediately pulled her shoulders back.

"Well? What are you waiting for?" Victoria demanded. "Go find this Noland character!"

Beatrice briefly looked from Clive to Henrietta as if for confirmation, but before either could give it, she dashed off as fast as she could go without actually running, which, Henrietta was pretty sure, would have given Victoria another reason to chastise the poor girl.

"Let's go have a look at this storage room while we're waiting," Clive suggested to Henrietta. He turned toward Victoria, who looked as though she was about to follow. "Mrs. Braithewaite, why don't you wait here for my mother? She'll be here shortly."

Mrs. Braithewaite seemed about to argue, but then, as if on second thought, she acquiesced and dropped back down into the armchair. "Yes, that's a very good idea, Clive." She wiped her forehead with a handkerchief. "I'm nearly at my wits' end. I'll order tea for us."

"Better make it for three," Henrietta inserted. "Sidney's coming, too."

Mrs. Braithewaite's face, already prone to frowning, frowned deeper. Sidney Bennett, Henrietta guessed, not origi-nally being of the gilded set, was probably about as welcome here as she herself had been back in the beginning when she had turned up on Clive's arm on the doorstep of Highbury wearing a borrowed busty dress from a fellow dancer at the Marlowe, her auburn hair piled high and an excessive amount of lipstick on her full lips. Poor Antonia, Henrietta thought now with a smile.

"Holly!" Victoria called now to a maid scurrying past with a large silver tray. "Tea for three! Oh, dear. Perhaps I should telephone Hugh. He'll be most upset." She began fanning herself again with the Christmas card.

"You'll excuse us, then," Clive said with a deferential tilt of his head.

"Yes, go on." Victoria gestured limply. "But come back as soon as you've found anything!"

Henrietta looped her arm through Clive's. "This way, Inspector. I'll show you where the storage room is. Doubtless you've never been in the back of the club where all the work is actually done."

"How perfectly condescending of you, Mrs. Howard. But I have once or twice mentioned my involvement in the war, have I not? A trench or two was dug. Plenty of mud and dysentery to go round."

"You don't fool me, darling. You were in the cavalry."

Clive let out what sounded like a cross between a grunt and a laugh as they rounded a corner and weaved through several staff members scurrying to and fro.

"Hugh's her husband, correct?" Henrietta asked, deciding it would be best to veer away from further banter about the war. She was surprised, in fact, that he had brought it up at all.

"Hugh?"

"Darling, do keep up. Yes, the Hugh Mrs. Braithewaite has mentioned several times now."

"Yes, her husband. Bit of a boob. Father couldn't stand him."

"I don't know if I've ever met him." Henrietta tried to remember him from the seemingly endless functions she had attended not only here at the club but at all of the private mansions to which they had been invited during their engagement and early marriage. In truth, she was getting the North Shore gilded set confused with the London aristocracy she was currently trying to memorize.

"You'd remember him. Short, balding, an air of presumption to him. Not all that intelligent, criminally dull."

"Well, that doesn't exactly narrow it down, Inspector. That describes exactly half the members."

"I take offense to that!"

She stopped now in front of a door with a brass plaque that read *Members of Staff* and patted his cheek. "I'm only joking, darling. Well, half joking. And, yes, exception granted in your case, as you're not really a member."

"Oh, good. For a moment I feared I might be 'criminally dull.'"

"That's one thing I would never accuse you of, Inspector," she said with a sly grin. "Shall we?"

Clive narrowed his eyes at her as he tried the door. It opened easily. He stepped inside the room, though it was really more a large closet than a room, per se. It was lined with wooden shelves holding a haphazard assortment of table linens, holiday decorations, wooden crates, some glassware, and what looked like a pile of lost-and-found items.

Clive held the door, examining the wood around the handle on both sides. "No sign of forced entry," he said almost to himself. "Which means it was either not locked or the culprit had the key. Where were the gifts stored?"

"Over in that corner," Henrietta nodded.

Clive walked over and began inspecting the nearby shelves and the floor.

Henrietta followed. "What are we looking for?" She rifled through a stack of thin towels.

"Something the culprit might have dropped, any type of clue." He glanced at her and seemed confused by her smile. "What is it?"

"Do you know how long it's been since you've uttered the word *clue*, Inspector?"

His perplexed face relaxed. "Listen, Minx," he said, suddenly putting his arms around her waist and pulling her close. "I'll have no more of your sauciness."

"Saucy?" she laughed. She put a finger to his lips, which he kissed. "Seems like old times, doesn't it?" she asked quietly. "I'm having flashbacks to the Marlowe."

"Except that we're not tied up and in danger of being killed any second."

"Well, yes, except that. But I do remember you said some very intimate things to me in that closet. Shocking, really, Inspector. I was just a young girl then."

"You weren't a young *girl*, you were a young woman. Which you still are now, I'll add. And, as I remember it, it was *you* that said something rather shockingly intimate to *me*."

"Well, I thought we were about to die."

"That's your excuse, is it?"

"Yes, it is," she said, running her finger along his lips again. "And here we are."

"Yes, here we are." His eyes darted around the room. "We've apparently moved up in the world, as now we're in the closet of a country club in Winnetka looking for a Christmas prankster instead of a serial killer in the underbelly of a burlesque club in Chicago."

"Well, you can't have everything."

Clive laughed and kissed her. "Have I told you lately that I love you?"

"Just this morning, I think."

Clive bent and kissed her again, this time deeply and long. Henrietta gripped his lapels and leaned into the kiss, her heart beginning to speed up in a dangerous sort of way, until she heard, "I do have other things to do, you know." Quickly she pulled back as a thin young man, followed closely by Beatrice, burst into the room.

"Oh! I beg your pardon," the steward said, looking from Clive to a flushed Henrietta. "You two the ones that want to see me?"

"Yes," Clive said, adjusting his tie. "I'm Clive Howard. This is my wife, Henrietta."

"Yeah, I remember you from yesterday," he said to her with a grin.

Henrietta merely raised a stern eyebrow.

"And you are?" Clive asked.

"Noland Peters. Day steward."

"You in charge?"

Noland let out a little sputter. "Nowhere near."

"Well, who is?"

"That'd be Mr. Cummings."

"And where is he?"

"Doesn't come in till one. On account he has to stay past midnight. Leaves the morning shift to ourselves."

"Seems odd," Clive mused.

"Listen, Noland," Henrietta said, deciding to redirect the interrogation. "May I call you Noland?"

The steward shrugged.

"Do you have any idea who would have taken the Christmas gifts we had stored here?"

"How should I know?" He scowled.

"When was the last time you saw the gifts?" Clive asked, taking over.

Noland thought for a minute. "S'pose when I locked up."

"And when was that?"

Noland shrugged again. "I don't know." His eyes flicked between Beatrice and Henrietta. "Ask one of them; they were here."

"Don't be smart."

"Why?" Noland grimaced. "I haven't done anything wrong. And who are you to question me, anyway?"

Clive bristled. "Someone who can make things very difficult for you." He took a step closer to him.

"Yeah? Like how?" Noland also took a step closer.

"Like I could have your job in a second, which I'm strongly considering doing regardless of whether I find you guilty or not."

"You don't have any authority over me!"

"Oh, yes, I do. Regardless of my standing at this club, I'm actually a detective. So, I suggest you start answering my, or my wife's, questions—*politely*—or I'll haul you off to the station and you can answer them there."

Noland's eyes grew wide. "Why didn't ya say you was a copper? How was I supposed to know?" he said, a slight whine in his voice now.

"I think it was about four-thirty, wasn't it Noland?" Henrietta interjected, throwing Clive a quick exasperated look. "I remember looking at my wristwatch because it was nearly Teddy's feeding time, and I was worried about getting back."

Noland took a step back, smoothing his hair with both hands. He nodded. "Yeah, I think that's right."

"Yes, and I remember that Mother and Charlotte and I left shortly thereafter because we had a reservation for tea at Chez Paul at five," Beatrice added quietly.

"Did you see anyone after they left?" Clive asked Noland.

"Just Miss MacKenzie. She came back in. Wanted to get back into the room. Said she lost something."

Clive's eyes flitted to Beatrice for confirmation.

"Oh . . . yes. I . . . I had forgotten. She was afraid she'd dropped a necklace, she said. But she was in and out very quickly. Mother was anxious that we not be late for our reservation."

"Did she find it?" Clive looked from Beatrice to Noland.

Noland shrugged. "Beats me."

"I don't think so," Beatrice answered meekly.

"Hmm." Clive rubbed his chin. "What time did *you* leave?" Clive asked Noland.

"Not until six. That's when I get off."

"Did you see anything suspicious?"

"Like someone carrying a load of gifts to a truck, maybe? No, not that I remember," he said sarcastically. "Look, I've told you all I know, which is nothing. I need to get back to work; I don't have all day to stand around and yap like some people."

"You'll stay here until I say otherwise," Clive snapped.

"Don't blow your wig, old man."

"Listen, sonny," Clive snarled, suddenly grabbing him by the jacket and shoving him up against the wall, "this is going to end with you getting socked in the mouth."

Beatrice let out a little scream.

"Go ahead!" Noland huffed, staring Clive in the eye. "That would be assault, and then I'd haul *you* down to the station."

"You little—"

"Clive!" Henrietta intervened, her heart racing. She hadn't seen him react this violently in a long, long time. Maybe it *was* better that he had given up detective work. "Let him go. This is silly."

"What is going on here!" shouted a portly man as he bustled into the room. "Mr. Peters! What is the meaning of this?" He turned to Clive then. "And what the hell do you think—" he stopped short. "Good heavens, Mr. Howard. Pardon me. What . . . what . . ." he glanced questioningly at Noland and then back to Clive. "I assume this is about the gifts, is it? I've just been informed." He hastily drew a handkerchief out of his pocket and mopped his forehead. "That's why I'm here early. Got a call mid-breakfast from a very angry Mrs. Braithewaite." He mopped his forehead again. "Which I did *not* appreciate, nor did Mrs. Cummings, I'll have you know. Always complaining that I practically live at this club, and here I am, proving her, for all intents and purposes, correct. Look, what's the meaning of this, Mr. Peters? There has to be some simple explanation."

"My thoughts exactly, Mr. Cummings," Clive interjected, "but your Mr. Peters here has not been the most accommodating, shall I say?"

"Whaddya mean? I answered all yer questions!"

"Under duress," Clive said with a scowl.

"See! He admits it! You heard him, Mr. Cummings! He said *duress*."

"Quiet, Peters. You'll do as you're told. Now, Mr. Howard, how can we assist? We're quite . . . anxious to keep this out of the press and to avoid involving the police." He gave a nervous chuckle. "I'm sure you understand."

"Hey! You said you *were* the police!" Noland exclaimed. "Dirty trick!"

"Peters! Hold your tongue!" Mr. Cummings commanded.

"On the contrary, I did not say that. I said I was a detective. And if we're being quite clear, I'm a private detective, and a former one."

"Mr. Cummings," Henrietta interjected, growing tired of this back-and-forth. "Who has keys to this storage room?"

"Well, myself, of course. Mr. Peters, and I believe Mrs. Braithewaite."

"That's all?" Clive's eyes narrowed. "Did you come into this room past six o'clock when Peters here left for the night?"

"No, I didn't," Mr. Cummings said somewhat defensively. "And it obviously wasn't Mrs. Braithewaite."

"Did you set your keys down at any point in the night? Long enough for someone to swipe them, open the door, and put them back before you noticed?"

Mr. Cummings thought hard. "I don't think so. I always keep them in my front vest pocket." He patted the bulging pocket.

"Did anyone see *you* leave, Peters?" Clive asked sternly.

"Hey! You don't think it was me, do you? What would I want with all that stuff?"

"Oh, I'm sure a young man of your ilk could think of several things to do with these items just before Christmas, and I don't mean giving them away to the needy. The contents would surely fetch a few bucks."

"That's . . . that's bonkers! I don't have to take this from you!"

"Or what? You'll quit?"

Noland's nostrils were flaring now and his chest heaving. "Yeah, I just might!"

"Well do it, then. My suggestion, Mr. Cummings, if you'll take my professional opinion, is to demand this clown's resignation if it is not volunteered."

"Surely Mr. Peters is not responsible for this theft, Mr. Howard! I can hardly believe it."

"Whether he's responsible or not, Mr. Cummings, I'd sack him anyway if I were in charge of staff. He's disrespectful, rude, and arrogant. We had men shot for less during the war."

"Well, the war's over, ain't it, old man? And all the old ways. This isn't Victorian England, ole chap," he sputtered in a horrible attempt at a British accent. "I've got just as many rights as you! Who do you think you are, anyway?"

"Peters! Silence. Report to my office. Now!" Mr. Cummings mopped his brow, looking oddly like Mrs. Braithewaite for one ridiculous moment. "I'm very sorry, Mr. Howard. "I will deal with this. I'll . . . I'll leave you to your investigation. We *are* very grateful for your assistance." He stuffed his handkerchief in his top pocket and hurried out.

Henrietta turned to Clive. "You were a little harsh on the poor boy, weren't you?"

"Harsh? Hardly. If Cummings doesn't end up firing him, I'll demand it."

"Clive," she stepped closer to him and tugged at his lapels again, "it's Christmas."

Clive let out a deep breath. "Well, as I'm not a full member of this club, I don't really have the power to fire anyone. But he's a cheeky little sod who should be put in his place. This would never happen in London, or even here in my father's day."

"Well," Henrietta said wistfully as she smoothed his jacket, "things change, as you're so fond of saying. It's a different world now."

He frowned. "Be that as it may, I'm sure he's involved, and now I'm more determined than ever to get to the bottom of this folly."

CHAPTER 6

"Three little kittens lost their mittens, and they began to cry!" chanted Doris and Donny as they held hands with Anna and danced around the plump tabby cat sitting contentedly on the antique Persian carpet, seemingly undisturbed by the high-pitched giggling surrounding her. She blinked lazily.

"Ashes, ashes, we all fall down!" they cried, mixing their nursery rhymes, and then fell to the floor, squealing with delight.

Elsie watched from across the room, where she sat embroidering. It hadn't taken her long to find Anna and the abducted cat in the garage at the end of the property, hiding under Karl's tool bench—Anna's current favorite hiding place. And though it broke Elsie's heart to do it, she had then promptly commanded that the three children bundle up and make inquiries at all of the houses surrounding the oval Palmer Square Park.

They had dutifully set off but had returned after only about twenty minutes, which, Elsie knew, was not even enough time to walk the whole perimeter of the park, much less stop at every house.

But by that point, it had grown dark, and she had given in to their pleadings to bring the cat in for the night and to take up the search in the morning. Meanwhile, they had decided to play with it, and, as Elsie bit a thread, watching, she was amazed to see how Anna was actually joining in with the other two, chanting the nursery rhymes along with them. She was responding to an animal faster than she had through any of Elsie's other methods of trying to teach her. Doris and Donny would start school next year, and it pained her to know that Anna, as an epileptic, would never get that chance. Thus, Elsie was all the more determined to teach her at home. She had already begun trying to teach her the alphabet, but it was slow going. Anna seemed either not willing or not capable of learning, but now, as Elsie saw her twirling and singing the songs she had so painstakingly tried to teach her, she wondered if perhaps they might keep the cat? Maybe it would be good for her . . .

But Ma, she knew, would not abide a cat. Hadn't she refused to let Elsie ever keep even one of the strays she had brought home throughout her childhood? But since Ma was stuck upstairs day after day, would she even know? She wondered what Gunther would say.

Almost as if on cue, she heard the front door open and close gently. "Hello," Gunther called. She heard him begin to remove his boots and his coat.

"We're in here!" Elsie called, setting aside her sewing.

Gunther strode into the room, his eyes going immediately to Elsie, and she felt a rush of love as she went to him. He gently took her hands in his and kissed her on the cheek, which still elicited a thrill in Elsie's heart, as they were, in truth, though so much had happened and though they already had such a full household, still newlyweds.

"Gunther! Look what Anna found!" Donny called, dispelling any further suggestion of romance.

Gunther let go of Elsie's hands and turned to look down at the children lying on the floor, their little heads propped in their hands, as they stared at the cat sitting in the middle of them.

"What is this?" he asked, crouching down. "*Eine Katze?*"

"Can we keep her?" Donny asked, sitting up on his knees. "Elsie said we could if you said yes."

Still crouched, Gunther twisted around to look at Elsie for confirmation of this pronouncement.

"That isn't exactly true, Donny," Elsie said quietly.

Gunther stood up, his knees cracking. Anna hurriedly stood, too, scooping the cat up in her arms and looking pleadingly at Gunther.

"This is strange problem, no?" He scratched the side of his head.

"She has a collar, so she must be lost," Elsie explained. "The children *say* they've asked through the neighborhood, but no one has claimed him—yet."

"But we did ask at all the houses!" Donny cried, jumping up.

"Kitty, Papa," Anna said in her fairy voice.

"*Liebling,*" he said, "we can't keep what isn't ours."

"But maybe whoever owned her doesn't want her anymore," Donny interjected. "Could we keep her then?"

"Yes, Gunther, can we?" Doris asked. She had gotten up, too, and was tugging at his jacket now.

Gunther gave her a reluctant smile as he tousled her brown curls. It was a sight that Elsie never grew tired of. Pa had died before the twins were even born, so they had never known a father, and Gunther had stepped so easily into that role. Doris, in particular, had warmed to him. She took his hand. "Can we?" she begged.

Gunther cleared his throat. "Well, I do not know. There is problem, you see, not just that she does not belong to us, but because I am allergic to cats." He shot an apologetic look at Elsie, and she felt her stomach sink. She hadn't realized how much she had been hoping, too . . .

"What's *'lergic*?" Donny asked.

"It is when something makes you sick—sneeze and cough. Some people are allergic to dogs, or trees, or flowers. Or cats."

"Well, maybe if you don't hold her?" Donny begged. "Then would you be 'lergic?"

Gunther looked at him sadly. "That is very good thinking. But I am afraid it does not work so easily that way. Bits of fur get into the air, you see." He rubbed his fingers together and then burst his hand wide open as if to demonstrate.

"Kitty?" Anna begged, holding the cat higher. Elsie wasn't sure if the girl had not understood what Gunther had just said or if it was a plea despite it. The fact that her big blue eyes had filled with tears suggested the latter.

Gunther sighed and pinched the bridge of his nose.

"That's enough now, children," Elsie said, giving her hands a brief clap. "It's time to wash up for dinner. I'll take the cat and put her on the back porch for now. Gunther and I will discuss it later." It was still difficult to know what to call Gunther in front of the children. Anna had called Gunther "Papa" from the time she was a baby, despite the fact that she was not his biological child, but it was confusing with Doris and Donny. Elsie and Gunther were like their parents, too, but they could hardly call Elsie *Mama*, as Anna did, since their mother was in fact sitting at this moment in a dark room upstairs. Elsie gently took the cat from Anna, who then grabbed hold of her skirt, and made a move toward the kitchen, Doris and Donny trailing beside her.

"Children!" Elsie turned to scold them. "I said to—"

The doorbell rang, interrupting her.

"I will go," Gunther announced. The task of answering the front door really should have fallen to Karl, the house's old manservant, but he was hopelessly hard of hearing and so dreadfully slow in making his way to the foyer that if the family waited for him to answer the door each time the bell rang, they would never have any visitors at all, as, after waiting for several long minutes, said visitors would assume there was no one at home and simply leave. Gunther had more than once mentioned having a word with Grandfather about letting old Karl "out to pasture," as it seemed a waste of Grandfather's money to continue to pay him a salary, but Elsie was loath to do so, knowing as she did that Karl was *already* pretty much out to pasture here in Palmer Square and indeed had nowhere else to go.

"Hello, may I help you?" Gunther asked, opening the door wide. Elsie handed the cat back to Anna and went to the door as well. She did not have a good feeling. On the stoop was a very old man bent with arthritis and leaning heavily on a cane. He wore no hat, and a burst of icy wind caused the only thin, gray lock of hair atop his head to stand upright.

"Do come in out of the cold," Elsie urged, wrapping her arms around herself against the chill.

The man hesitated a moment and then shuffled forward. "Just for a minute, like," he mumbled with what Elsie guessed might be a slight Scottish accent. He wore no gloves, and his crippled hands looked raw and red from exposure, and his coat, Elsie observed, was very thin and even ripped in a couple of spots. "Thank ye kindly." He addressed them as best he could with his rounded back—twisting his neck upwards and peering at them with one eye. "I've been out a while, you see. 'Fore the snow."

"Snow?" Elsie looked out of one of the leaded glass panels. Despite the cold temperature, the evening sky was clear.

"Me knee's been achin' terrible all day. Gonna snow, all right." He leaned heavily on his cane.

"Would you like to sit down?" Elsie asked, throwing Gunther a sideways look.

"Yes, please. Sit down and warm yourself." Gunther gestured toward the front parlor.

"No, no. I can't stay long. I'm out looking for me cat. Went missing, he did."

Elsie's heart sank. A loud meow was heard then, and a thud, which was presumably the cat jumping out of Anna's arms, who, Elsie was pretty sure, was hiding around the corner with Doris and Donny, listening.

"Tom!" the old man cried as the cat trotted straight for him. "Oh, Tom! You naughty bugger! Whatareya doin' *here*?"

The cat rubbed against the old man's leg.

"Thank ye kindly fer findin' 'im!" The man looked from Gunther to Elsie. "I hope he weren't no trouble."

"Not at all, Mr. . . . ?"

"Ferguson. Bob Ferguson."

"You're sure you don't want to sit down, Mr. Ferguson? Warm up for a few moments?" Elsie asked, swallowing her disappointment. But, on the other hand, the current development spared her and Gunther from having to make a hard decision. She felt Anna grip the back of her skirt. She must have slunk out of her hiding place, not unlike a cat herself. Doris and Donny silently appeared now as well, Donny's face sullen.

"No, no. Irene'll be missing me. No," he said, twisting his neck up again. "I need ta go. Want ta be home 'fore it gets too late. Irene worries, ya see."

"Do you have far to go? Are you on the Square?" Elsie asked. By the look of him, he didn't seem like someone that could afford a house on Palmer Square, but Elsie, more than anyone, knew that appearances could be deceiving.

"Nah. Used to live here on the Square, but don't no more. Near, though." He turned and shuffled toward the door. The cat dashed in front of him and stood at the door, looking up eagerly at his owner and ready to bolt.

"Dang it, Tom. Don't you go runnin' out now. That's what happened afore, you see. I opened the door, and out he runs. By the time I gets me coat, he was long gone. Don' know what's gotten inta him lately."

"I'll go with you and carry Tom," Gunther said, reaching for his thick wool coat from the coat stand. "We don't want him dashing off again." He wrapped his scarf around his neck and sneezed.

"No," Elsie said firmly. "I'll go. *I'll* carry Tom. If you do, you'll be miserable all night. I can already see your eyes beginning to water." Elsie quickly slipped into her coat and then scooped up Tom in her arms before Gunther could do so. "No more straying for you, young man!" she said, giving the cat a little pet.

"Mama!" Anna said in a high-pitched cry. Elsie's heart clenched a little. She turned and crouched down in front of the girl. "Now, look, Anna. Tom, here, has got to go home. He's missing his bed and his mama. He's had a lovely time here with us, haven't you, Tom? And maybe someday we can go and visit, if that's all right with Mr. Ferguson." She glanced over her shoulder at the old man, but he had either not heard her, not understood, or simply not wanted the children to come visit, as he just stared back at Elsie, his cloudy eyes a blank. She turned back to Anna.

"Go on, give him a little pet."

Doris and Donny gave the cat several long pets, Doris kissing him on the head. "Oh, Tom! I'm sorry we thought you were a girl. We'll miss you!"

Anna did not reach out to pet the cat but instead buried her face in his fur and then tried to pull him out of Elsie's arms.

"Anna, say good-bye now." Elsie said, trying to stand up straight. Anna remained glued to the cat, however, until Gunther came and pulled her gently away. He picked her up and held the now crying girl in his arms, sneezing again as he did so.

"Ask Nanny to come down and get them washed," Elsie instructed. "And tell Chef to begin dinner. Don't wait for me. I'll be back in a bit."

"Be careful, *Liebling*," Gunther said above Anna's wails. Though Elsie's heart was breaking for the three little kittens before her, she forced herself to turn away from them. It wouldn't do to show any emotion, lest the three of them break down further, especially the littlest kitten in Gunther's arms, who had lost more than her mittens many times over.

CHAPTER 7

The morning of the Christmas Ball dawned, and still the club Christmas gifts were missing. Predictably, Antonia was in a very sour mood at breakfast, though Henrietta tried to cheer her by turning the discussion to Julia's imminent arrival in just a few days' time, but to no avail. Not so easily thwarted, Henrietta had then suggested that perhaps the two of them drive into town to do some Christmas shopping, but that, too, had fallen on deaf ears. Antonia seemed almost offended that she would suggest something so trivial at "a time like this" and instead excused herself to dash off to the club for an emergency meeting of the committee, but not before expressing to Clive how disappointed she was in him for not immediately solving "the case," as she was calling it.

"I don't know what more she wants of me," Clive said irritably once they were back upstairs in their private sitting room. "It's impossible to solve a case in a day."

Indeed, after their interrogation of Noland Peters, Mr. Cummings, and various other staff members, they were no closer to understanding who had taken the gifts or why, beyond the obvious—that they had been stolen in order to sell the items inside. No one seemed to have seen or heard anything unusual—no strange delivery trucks, no sign of any forced entry on any of the doors. It remained a mystery.

Henrietta, while certainly concerned about the missing gifts as well as Clive's continued peevishness, was in truth more focused at the moment on watching Teddy's attempts to crawl. Currently, he was up on his hands and knees, rocking, but he had yet to sally forth.

"Obviously, someone had to see something. We just need more time to question the staff. It doesn't seem like an outside job." Clive ran a hand roughly through his hair and wandered to the windows.

"Well, why don't you use the time tonight to secretly question the staff? They'll be busy and distracted and therefore maybe more inclined to let something slip."

"Yes, I'd thought of that, too. But even if we do figure out who did it, it's unlikely we'll ever get the gifts back now, so it hardly matters."

Henrietta scooped up Teddy, thereby ending his attempt at mobility, and joined Clive at the window. "Where's your sense of justice and all of that?" she said with a wry smile. "Isn't that what you used to always go on about?"

"Are you mocking me?" he asked. He held out a finger to Teddy, who gripped it tightly. Teddy then leaned his little body toward Clive, who easily took him into his arms and let him pat his face with his little hand.

"I wouldn't dream of it, darling. And I'm not trying to take your mother's side, but I think the bigger concern, besides finding the culprit, of course, is what to do about the poor, especially the children. Did you really mean it, that we would front the cash for new gifts?"

"Of course I did," he mumbled, Teddy having taken hold of his bottom lip. "Sidney's working on it now behind the scenes."

"Speaking of, did you have a chance to apologize to him?"

"Yes, yes. He was very forgiving, of course, said not to give it another thought, but it has been a bit chillier between us."

"Well, I hope he can figure something out. If not, maybe Victoria already has a plan in place. Despite what Antonia says, I do think we could redo all the packages. They might not get delivered as scheduled, but maybe by Christmas Eve."

"Yes, maybe," Clive agreed absently.

"And now, I really need to be on my way, or I'll never get my own shopping done. I've a horribly long list! Oh, why don't you come with me?" Teddy was leaning toward her now, so she took him back into her arms and walked with him toward her bedroom.

"As much as I'd like to trudge down Elm jostling my way between the crowds scurrying in and out of shops to make last-minute purchases, getting my toes stepped on and my sides poked," Clive called, following her, "I really must decline. I promised Sidney that I would inspect the stables' apartments with him this afternoon."

"You will be civil, won't you?"

"Yes, yes, I will, darling. You needn't instruct me."

Henrietta sighed and set Teddy down on the immense four-poster bed. "Well, I'll just have to go alone, I suppose. It's too bad I can't take Edna."

"Why don't you?"

Henrietta nodded at Teddy.

"You know, you *could* leave him with Nanny for a few hours. It won't hurt him."

"Clive! The woman's about a hundred years old, in case you haven't noticed. And I won't subject poor Teddy to what will probably be an afternoon crying his eyes out in a crib and being given a dose of cod-liver oil or some other strange concoction!"

Clive laughed. "True enough."

Henrietta, however, was not amused, and crossed her arms. "Maybe I should take him and Edna with me."

"Darling, that's ridiculous." He came over and put his arms around her. "If you really want me to go, I will. I'll tell Sidney the renovation can wait."

Teddy flopped onto his back then, rolled over, and began crawling dangerously close to the edge of the bed. Clive broke free of their embrace and grabbed him back into his arms. "Got you!"

Teddy squealed with delight.

Henrietta laughed. "Good catch. No, you go on. Meet with Sidney. If I buy too many things, I'll simply arrange for them to be delivered."

"Tell you what. If I finish early, I'll meet you in town." Clive shifted Teddy onto his shoulder. "How about—"

He was interrupted, then, by a quick knock and the sudden opening of the door. Antonia barged in but stopped midstep, staring at Clive as if she were seeing a ghost.

"What on earth are you doing?" she demanded. "Is something wrong?" She looked at Henrietta as if for an answer and then back at Clive. "Why are you holding the baby?" Her voice was one of almost panic.

"Well, he *is* my child, Mother," Clive drawled, rolling his eyes.

Antonia's arched shoulders relaxed. "In my day, men didn't hold babies, or children, for that matter. Your father didn't hold you until you were two years of age."

"Yes, I'm aware, Mother." Clive kissed Teddy's head, as if to taunt her.

Antonia frowned.

"You're back early, Antonia. Any news about the gifts?" Henrietta tried to ask cheerfully.

"Heavens, yes! That's why I came up here in the first place. The gifts have been found!" she declared triumphantly, as if she herself had discovered them.

"They have? That's wonderful! Where were they?" Henrietta reached for Teddy, and Clive released him.

"That's the oddest thing! They turned up back in the storage room, exactly where they had been before."

"Have you examined them?" Clive tugged at his ear. "Are you sure they're the same gifts?"

"The same gifts? Of course, they're the same gifts! Victoria actually opened one and found everything as originally packed."

"But did she check them all? Some of them might have been tampered with. Maybe even be empty."

"Oh, Clive, you *are* tiresome. Can't we just be happy that the gifts are back and that Christmas has been saved?"

"Well, even if all of the gifts *do* still hold their original contents, we don't know who took them or why. Doesn't that bother you?"

"Yes, I suppose. But I'm assuming your early theory is probably the correct one. Just a silly prank. There seems to be no other explanation. And we haven't time to figure it out."

"I'm not so sure," Clive mused.

"You had your chance to play the detective, Clive, but it's too late now. We don't have time to open them all and rewrap them! Victoria and I have decided to go ahead with the delivery as scheduled."

"That's foolish, Mother. Anything could be in those gifts!"

"Like what? A bomb? Rocks? Honestly, Clive, I should never have asked you to get involved in the first place. You only complicate things!"

Teddy began to fuss now, and Henrietta swayed her hips, trying to rock him, though she guessed it wouldn't help. He was either upset by the sudden tension in the room or hungry, or maybe both.

"Well, I'll leave you to it." Antonia threw an irritated look in Teddy's direction. "I can't abide a crying baby, and I have so very much to do."

Clive opened his mouth to respond, but Antonia exited before he could do so.

"You're not going to let it go, are you?" Henrietta asked him over Teddy's fussing.

"Not a chance," he said grimly. "My guess is that Peters returned the gifts in a feeble attempt to get his job back."

"But why would he do that? If I were him, I'd cut my losses and try to sell the gifts. Bringing them back wouldn't induce the club to give him his job back, would it?"

"No, I suppose not."

"*And*, we don't even know for sure if Mr. Cummings really did fire Noland. Perhaps he didn't."

"Ugh." Clive walked back to the window, reaching for the pipe in his pocket as he did so. "If only we didn't have to attend this silly ball. Mother parading us about as if we're royalty."

"Well, I suppose we are, really. I seem to remember you snapping at Randolph one night that you're the twelfth in line to the British throne or some such thing, and you've moved up the line a few steps since. What are you now? Tenth?"

"Don't be ridiculous."

"And don't forget that *I'm* the Countess of Koenig," she laughed, referring to a misunderstanding, to put it nicely, that had occurred with her distant uncle, Baron Von Harmon, while they were on a case in Strasbourg.

"Now you're just being silly."

"Well, I do wonder what's become of Castle Freudeneck, as it seems that all of my distant relatives have died out. Perhaps the disgraced American branch of the Von Harmons will inherit it, though I suppose that means it would go to Eugene," she mused.

"Are you *quite* finished?"

"I suppose," she said over Teddy's fussing, which had elevated to a lusty cry now. "And royalty or not, this little boy needs feeding."

CHAPTER 8

"Smile!" shouted a man as Henrietta stepped out of the Rolls. A flash of light exploded in front of her, and she instinctively put her hand in front of her face. When she lowered it, she saw a photographer crouching a few feet in front of her, his camera still poised at his eye.

"Another, Lady Linley!"

Without thinking, Henrietta obliged.

"That's it. Now one with Lord Linley," he called as Clive came around and took her arm. Clive did *not* pose, however, and instead guided Henrietta into the club, the photographer's bulb continuing to flash behind them.

"Why are there reporters here?" Henrietta whispered, leaning into Clive.

"Probably Mother's doing. Wanting us in the society papers."

"Be nice," she muttered as a steward stepped forward to take her white ermine stole. She patted the diamond necklace

Alcott and Antonia had given her as an engagement present last year. It sparkled beautifully on her creamy neck, accentuating her bare shoulders and complementing the diamond tiara that Edna had expertly arranged in her auburn hair. Henrietta smoothed her scarlet Vionnet gown and looked about her.

"I'm always nice, darling," Clive said gruffly, adjusting his cufflinks.

"No, you're not. But you can do this for your mother."

Clive let out another grunt and began weaving them through the already sizable crowd loitering and chatting in the gathering room. The lights had been dimmed and what looked like hundreds of candles lit, all of which reflected the gold tinsel on the massive tree. Strains of a jazzy version of "Winter Wonderland" wafted in from the ballroom beyond, and Henrietta couldn't help but feel excited in the festive elegance around her. She had always loved Christmas!

"Are *those* the gifts?" Henrietta asked, peering through the dim light at the swath of presents arranged prettily under the tree. "Yes, I'm *sure* they are. I recognize the wrapping. But why are they out here?" She shot Clive a questioning look.

"They do this every year. Display them under the tree during the ball so that the esteemed members feel as though they've done their good deed for Christmas. Makes all of the champagne and the caviar hors d'oeuvres go down easier, you see."

"But is it wise to just leave them lying in the open like that?" Henrietta asked, deciding to ignore his commentary. "They've already been stolen once."

Clive gave a little shrug. "I was not consulted, darling. And God forbid they break with tradition."

Henrietta faced him, very tempted to pinch his cheek, but she resisted, as it would be unladylike in the extreme, so she settled for a scolding. "You're very ambiguous when it comes to the question of tradition, aren't you? You champion it only when it suits."

He gave her an infuriating little wink.

"Oh, you look lovely, Henrietta!" Antonia gushed as she hurried toward them now. "Doesn't she, Clive?"

"She's always lovely." His gaze held Henrietta's as the corner of his mouth wickedly curled and one eyebrow raised.

"Yes, but you know what I mean. Honestly, Clive. Now, come this way," Antonia urged. "We've been waiting to start the dancing. I do hope you posed for the photographers." Without waiting for them to reply, she gave a nod across the room to Mr. Cummings, who then began politely addressing the groups of people scattered about, gesturing as he did so toward the ballroom. Slowly, people began to migrate. Almost all the ladies, Henrietta noticed, were either in red, green, black, or cream gowns. The men, of course, were all in white tie, including Clive, whom she thought looked unusually handsome tonight.

Antonia led them over to the bandstand, where Victoria Braithewaite, tightly wrapped in a gown of silver sequins, was waiting, her usual deep frown creasing her face. Henrietta tried to remember if she had ever seen Victoria genuinely smile.

"Good evening, Mrs. Braithewaite," Clive said pleasantly as they approached.

"Good evening," the older woman responded with a nod. "You're looking well, Clive. Marriage agrees with you," she sniffed.

"Thank you."

"It's wonderful about the gifts, isn't it, Mrs. Braithewaite?" Henrietta asked. Antonia had stepped a few paces away and was now engaged in a whispered conversation with the bandleader. "I mean, that they've been returned."

"Yes. Thank goodness! I don't know what could have possibly happened to them. But they're back now, and that's all that matters." She mopped her forehead with her handkerchief as she looked out over the crowd. "Have you had any luck in discovering who was responsible, Clive?" She peered at him.

"No, but I hope to."

"Well, I suppose it doesn't matter now," she said with a heavy sigh. "It was obviously a joke. A very bad one, I daresay. But I *would* like to see the guilty party punished for the distress it has caused me. A whole afternoon in bed!" she lamented. "My guess is that it was one of these impertinent stewards. Or a disgruntled cook, perhaps. Do we not pay them enough? I blame the war, you know!"

The bandleader signaled his musicians, then, who proceeded to neatly wrap up the piece they were playing—"Love Is the Sweetest Thing," if Henrietta wasn't mistaken. The bandleader covered the tall silver microphone with one hand and leaned toward Antonia, again whispering something to her. She nodded and patted her hair.

"Ladies and gentlemen, quiet please!" the bandleader announced. "Quiet! Just for a moment." He held up his hands and then paused, waiting for the aimless chatter in the vaulted ballroom to subside. "Ladies and gentlemen," he repeated, his thin pencil moustache unmoving despite his pursed lips, "the organizer of tonight's gala would like a few words. So it is with great pleasure that I give you . . . Mrs. Sidney Bennett." He gestured at Antonia and then proceeded to lead the crowd in a gentle round of clapping.

Antonia took hold of the microphone pole and looked out proudly over the crowd, savoring this moment as if she had been waiting for it all her life. The crowd was attentive.

"Merry Christmas! Thank you all for coming out for what has become our annual Christmas Ball, which dates back to the very founding of the club in 1882."

Several people clapped.

"And as you know, a part of that tradition is to collect gifts for the poor of our community. This year has been no exception, and I'm pleased to announce that we are able to provide fifty-six Christmas boxes this year." There was another round of quiet applause. "Thank you to Mrs. Hugh Braithewaite for spearheading the committee this year." She gestured limply at Victoria, and the crowd gave an even weaker round of claps. "Now!" Her eyes were bright as she looked out over the crowd. "I have something very special—"

She was interrupted in her address, however, by Victoria herself, who bustled forward as quickly as her sequined body would allow and brazenly took hold of the microphone pole, perhaps misunderstanding Antonia's acknowledgement and instead perceiving it as an invitation to speak. Antonia, however, seemed bewildered by her "friend's" actions and also kept hold of the pole, so that for several embarrassing moments, both women held it, pulling at it slightly, until Antonia finally released her grip.

"Mrs. Hugh Braithewaite," she announced to the crowd with a thin smile, though—without the aid of the microphone's amplification—her voice fell flat.

Mrs. Braithewaite, however, her expansive chest heaving slightly from the effort of wresting the microphone, did not seem to mind the muted introduction in the slightest.

"Thank you!" she said loudly into the microphone, causing it to screech. She took a step back. "Thank you," she repeated gingerly, trying to avoid another screech. "Thank you all for your very generous contributions this year. I'm sure the less fortunate in our community will be most appreciative. Despite what I will call a small inconvenience," she glanced disapprovingly at Clive, as if *he* were somehow responsible, "we have been very successful. It is each of you that makes our club so special, so intrinsic to the greater community. So please do enjoy yourselves tonight, and I hope each and every one of you have a blessed, happy Christmas!"

There was a cheery round of applause.

"And so . . . it is my very great pleasure to open this year's Chrrrriiiistmas Ball!!" she pronounced loudly and threw open her arms. The crowd clapped heartily now, various persons shouting *Merry Christmas!* across the ballroom. As if on cue, the band began to play.

"But wait!" Antonia cried, a look of horror on her face. She grabbed the microphone back and pierced Victoria with a look of fury. The music warbled and then came to an uneven halt. "Please," she said, her lips nearly touching the microphone in her panic, causing another unfortunate screech. "Just one more announcement!" she said, moving back slightly and giving Victoria another glare. "I also wanted to announce . . . to announce . . ." she faltered and paused, as if trying to remember what had probably been a more eloquent speech.

She took a deep breath and began again. "We have two very special guests with us tonight! All the way from London to open our Christmas Ball!" Her eyes darted rapidly around the room. "You might know them as my son and daughter-in-law, Clive and Henrietta Howard, but tonight I have the great pleasure to introduce them as . . . Lord and Lady Linley!" she announced with as much flourish as she could manage, but the proclamation did not seem to have its desired effect, either because the crowd had already tired of clapping, or because Victoria's speech had rendered Antonia's to be anticlimactic (very likely), or because the band had now begun playing their first waltz of the night, as previously arranged.

Despite the muted reception, Clive stepped forward on cue, gave Henrietta an elegant bow, and took her hand in his. Stiffly, he led her to the dance floor, paused for several seconds as he waited for the right beat, and then began to expertly twirl her.

Henrietta waited until they were in a bit of a rhythm and then leaned her head very close to his. "I know you don't have sympathy for your mother," she said into his ear, "but Victoria Braithewaite can be an absolute crumb."

"Indeed. Had you not noticed before now, darling?" he asked wryly.

"It makes me not even care about the theft."

"Now you're catching on." He twirled her again.

"Remember to smile," Henrietta advised once she was back in his arms.

"I *am* smiling, darling."

"No, you're not. You're grimacing."

"Same thing."

"No, it's a different thing altogether. You look as though you have indigestion."

"I *do* have indigestion."

She stifled a laugh as he twirled her again. Several other couples joined them then, filling the space. When the waltz finished, Lord and Lady Linley broke apart, whereupon a small crowd gathered around Henrietta, mostly men wanting to ask her for the next dance. With a teasing little wink, Clive backed away as Henrietta was quickly led back to the dance floor, her new partner none other than Hugh Braithewaite. She threw a final glance at Clive, whom, she knew, would be seeking out Mrs. Braithewaite, as would be expected of him. And after that dance, he would be obliged to ask various other prominent ladies to accompany him until he could find a chance to slip away unnoticed.

Henrietta turned her gaze to Mr. Braithewaite, whom, she observed, was staring intently at her diamond necklace . . . or maybe it was her cleavage. Henrietta sighed. The music began, and she put one hand on his shoulder as he placed one on her back, a little lower than she was comfortable with. He began to clumsily lead her.

There were several uncomfortable minutes of silence between them (not counting his heavy breathing) during which Mr. Braithewaite seemed to be concentrating on his steps. Henrietta wished he would speak to make the dance go faster, as it was not her place, she knew, to begin any conversation.

"Fine weather we're having, is it not?" he finally asked with what seemed to be inflamed sinuses. That, or he was naturally nasal.

Oh, dear. Not the weather. "One might say so, Mr. Braithewaite. But I must admit, I was rather hoping it would snow for Christmas. Weren't you?"

"Snow? Don't mind either way. All the same to me."

"We don't get much snow in London, more up toward Derbyshire. Plenty of rain, though."

"Yes, it was that way when I was at Cambridge. Did you know I was at Cambridge?" He looked at her keenly.

"No, I didn't."

"Well, I was. That's where I met your father-in-law."

"Really? I thought you met here, after Alcott came over to marry Antonia."

"No, I had met him at Cambridge. We were in a couple of different clubs together. Never best friends, you know. He ran with a different set altogether, all the sons of lords and dukes. Not quite my speed. But still."

"I see. It's a small world, I suppose."

There were several more uncomfortable moments of silence then, during which Henrietta looked over his shoulder to try to locate Clive or perhaps Charlotte MacKenzie. She would like to ask her a few questions. Her initial sweep of the room, however, yielded nothing.

"There has been quite a bit of rain here, too, though, this month."

Henrietta sighed and wondered if he knew how boring he was. She looked at him and was annoyed that his gaze had gravitated back to her chest. She was used to being ogled by men, but they were usually not *this* obvious. She was tempted to tap his chin to get his eyes to look at hers.

"Did Miss MacKenzie come with you tonight?" she asked, trying to distract him.

"Charlotte?" He looked up, his eyes bright. "But of course she did. Capital girl. Just what Beatrice needs, you know. Kind of like an older sister."

"But are they not the same age?"

Mr. Braithewaite cleared his throat. "That may be, but Charlotte *seems* older. Comports herself well, you see."

"It was very kind of her to come and stay with you, considering it's Christmas. I'd have thought she would want to be with her family."

Mr. Braithewaite grunted. "Off in Bucharest at the moment. Brother in trouble or some such thing. Gambling, I think it was. Charlotte, of course, had no desire to tag along on what was essentially designed to be a rescue mission, so Victoria offered to host her for the holidays. Couldn't have worked out better. She's just what the house needed—a breath of fresh air."

The dance thankfully ended then, and Mr. Braithewaite released her, but not before "accidentally" brushing his hand along the side of her breast.

Henrietta bristled but smiled politely through gritted teeth.

"Thank you for the dance, Mrs. Howard. Or I suppose I should say *Lady Linley*." He leered at her.

Henrietta had to fight the urge to roll her eyes.

"Perhaps you'll stand up with me for another later on?" he asked in a gravelly voice.

"But of course, Mr. Braithewaite. And now if you'll excuse me."

She moved away from him, hoping to get a chance to look for Charlotte, but she didn't get far before a Mr. Marcus Wilcox stepped in front of her and asked for the next dance. With a sigh, she took his hand and was led, rather expertly, she had to admit, around the dance floor to another of Strauss's waltzes. Next came a Mr. Erastus Patterson, then a Mr. Joseph Armor, and finally a Mr. Chadwick Field, until enough time had passed that it was finally excusable to beg leave to powder her nose.

Henrietta slipped out of the ballroom and retreated back to the gathering room. She quickly perused it, looking for Clive or Charlotte, but she did not spot either of them. She decided to remain, however, thinking that this might be her chance to inspect the gifts under the tree. She crept closer, trying not to make eye contact with any of the other people loitering around the room, chattering in small groups. An occasional booming laugh erupted here and there, or else a twittering giggle from one of the society ladies.

When Henrietta reached the tree, she stood before it as if simply admiring it. But then, with a quick look over her shoulder, she bent and picked up one of the gifts. She turned it this way and that. It *felt* to be the same original weight—if she remembered correctly. But would they all? She didn't think she had time to pick up and judge all fifty-six. But surely whoever had moved them from the storage room to the tree would have noticed if one—or many—of them were empty, wouldn't they? She wondered if it had been Noland's job to move them all.

She picked up another box and inspected it. It was the same wrapping paper, she was sure, but she did notice, upon careful examination, that the cellophane had been tampered with in several places. But perhaps, she mused, setting it back down, this was the one Victoria had unwrapped. Henrietta picked up another and saw that this one, too, had signs of having been unwrapped and rewrapped. Had Victoria unwrapped more than one?

Henrietta moved toward the back of the tree and picked up another . . . and another . . . and still another. Nearly every package she picked up showed signs of being tampered with. But why? Clive's suspicion that someone had replaced the contents seemed more and more likely, and yet the package that Victoria happened to have opened contained the original items. What were the chances of that?

Henrietta glanced back toward the ballroom and noticed Charlotte MacKenzie standing on the periphery. Just the person! Henrietta set down the package she was holding, but by the time she looked back, Charlotte had disappeared.

Henrietta hesitated, knowing that as soon as she stepped foot back in the ballroom, she would be asked to dance. She stood, considering for several moments, and finally decided she would just have to risk it. She edged closer to the dance floor and perched herself behind a very tall young man in hopes of remaining inconspicuous. She perused the floor. She did not see Clive, which meant, hopefully, that he had slipped away to conduct his own interrogations. Unfortunately, she did not see Charlotte, either. Where could she have gone?

Henrietta stepped further out from behind the tall man and looked again, this time spotting the girl in a far corner talking with Mr. Braithewaite. Poor thing. She would rescue her.

Henrietta quickly weaved her way through the crowd, trying her best not to catch anyone's eyes until she safely reached the captor and his latest prey.

"Ah. Mrs. Howard," Mr. Braithewaite droned as Henrietta approached. "Come to claim your dance, have you?"

Henrietta bit the inside of her cheek. "Not just yet." She flashed him a small smile. "But I would be ever so grateful for a glass of punch." She forced herself to bat her eyes slightly. "Wouldn't you, Charlotte?"

Charlotte seemed surprised by this suggestion, but gave a small nod, whereupon Mr. Braithewaite snapped to attention.

"But of course!" He gave an exaggerated bow. "I will return in a moment!"

He hurried away, and Henrietta promptly turned to Charlotte, whose eyes were following Mr. Braithewaite as he disappeared into the crowd.

"Charlotte, is everything all right? You look pale. Are you ill?"

Charlotte pulled her gaze back to Henrietta. "No, not at all. I'm perfectly fine. How lovely you look tonight," she added politely.

Henrietta peered at the young woman in front of her. Something seemed amiss. Gone was the bubbly young woman she had met the other day. Perhaps she was simply missing her family? Maybe this wasn't the right time to question her . . .

However, she knew she might not get another chance. "Charlotte, I came to ask you if you knew anything about the gifts being taken yesterday," she asked in a low voice, deciding to plow ahead.

"Me? No." Charlotte's brow was furrowed. "Why?"

"Because I think you might have been the last person to see the gifts when you went back to look for your necklace."

Charlotte's hand went to her chest. "How . . . how did *you* know about my necklace?"

"The steward told us."

"Us?" she asked worriedly.

"Yes, my husband and I are—" Henrietta paused before using the word *investigating*—"looking into it."

Charlotte's brow furrowed further. "Looking into what?" Her hand remained on her chest.

"The missing gifts."

Charlotte let out what a little breath of what seemed to be relief. "Oh." She was silent for a moment. "But why? They're back, aren't they?"

"Well, yes, but I suppose we'd still like to figure out who did it."

"Oh," Charlotte mused. "I see."

"So, you lost a necklace? Funny, but I don't remember you wearing a necklace that day."

Charlotte's face went from white to pink in an instant. "I wear it inside my dress," she explained hastily. "The clasp is faulty. I've been meaning to get it repaired, but I just haven't had time. I wear it inside my dress in case it breaks, but I guess it didn't help. It must have somehow slipped through my dress."

"Is it valuable?"

Charlotte's cheeks flushed again. "Valuable? Well, no." She paused. "I'm not entirely sure, actually. It has more sentimental value to me. It was a gift, you see, from . . . from my brother."

Henrietta turned this over. *If the necklace was such a sentimental piece, why chance wearing it with a faulty clasp?* "When did you realize it was missing?"

"Just as I was getting into the car with Mrs. Braithewaite and Beatrice. I begged a moment's leave and ran back to the Chesapeake Room and searched everywhere, but to no avail. Then I thought to look in the storage room, thinking maybe it had slipped off there. As you said, the steward let me in."

"Did you open any of the boxes?" Henrietta asked eagerly, thinking that this might be the answer to at least part of the mystery.

"Open them? No, why would I have . . . ? Oh! I see! You think it could have fallen inside one of the boxes? Oh, I never thought of that!" Her eyes flicked toward the gathering room. "Well, even if I *had* thought of it, I hadn't time. Mrs. Braithewaite was already angry with me by the time I got back out to the car. Never mind that we were still a full fifteen minutes early for our reservation at Chez Paul. She . . ." Charlotte hesitated, ". . . she can be . . . difficult sometimes."

Henrietta rather thought that Victoria Braithewaite could be difficult *all* of the time, but she didn't say so. "Did you report it to anyone? Mr. Cummings, perhaps?"

"No, I didn't see him." She paused, as if trying to remember. "It was just the steward I told, I think."

Henrietta thought for a moment. "Have you found it?"

Charlotte shook her head morosely. "No, I haven't."

"What did it look like? I'll keep my eye out for it."

"It's a . . . a gold pendant," she said slowly. "On the front is a cross with a diamond in the middle, and on the back is a crest . . . with a spade in it I think, and maybe a stalk of corn?"

"How unusual."

"Well, as I said, it was my . . . my brother's."

"The one in Bucharest?"

Charlotte's eyes opened wide. "How did you know he was in Bucharest?"

"Mr. Braithewaite mentioned it to me."

"What did he say about him?" she asked urgently.

"Just that your family was there visiting him," Henrietta fibbed, deciding not to elaborate on the gambling debts or that he might be in trouble.

Charlotte's face remained pensive, as if she were thinking this through.

Henrietta glanced over her shoulder and could see Mr. Braithewaite carefully winding his way back through the crowd, a cup of punch in each hand. She tried to think of any last questions. "Did Noland relock the room after you left?"

Charlotte did not answer; her eyes seemed to be following Mr. Braithewaite, too.

"Charlotte?"

The young woman shook her head and looked back at Henrietta. "I beg your pardon?"

"Did the steward relock the room?"

Charlotte blinked, trying to remember. "I can't say. I left in such a hurry, you see."

"Here we are!" boomed Mr. Braithewaite. "Two punches!" He handed one to Henrietta and then to Charlotte, his gaze lingering not on Henrietta, but on Charlotte! Henrietta felt her stomach clench. Surely, Hugh Braithewaite would not attempt to seduce this young woman, who was not only a guest in his home but the daughter of his wife's friend—not to mention the fact that he was about forty years older than her? The thought was repulsive, and yet . . . if she wasn't mistaken, it seemed that Charlotte was oddly returning his look. The poor girl! She must be horribly misguided! Who would possibly find Hugh Braithewaite in the slightest bit attractive?

She needed to find Clive.

"You'll excuse me, won't you?" she said to both of them, who were still staring at each other.

"Yes, of course," Mr. Braithewaite grunted, pulling his attention away from Charlotte. "But don't forget you owe me a dance, Mrs. Howard!"

Henrietta did not answer but weaved through the crowd on the edges of the room, declining two offers to dance as she went and wondering if there *was* something between Mr. Braithewaite and Charlotte, or if Hugh was really just a lecherous old fool.

"There you are, darling!" Clive said, suddenly appearing at her side. "I've been looking for you everywhere. Everything all right? You look flushed."

"I'm perfectly fine. But I've made a bit of a discovery."

"Me, too." He raised an eyebrow. "You first."

"Let's go out where it's quieter. And perhaps a bit cooler. It's so stuffy in here."

Clive led her into the gathering room and took up a stance in one of the dark corners not far from the tree. He leaned a shoulder on the paneled wood and crossed his arms. "Spill it, sister," he said in a gangster voice.

Henrietta let out a little laugh and stepped around him. "Well, in the first place, I've discovered that most of the gifts, maybe *all* of the gifts, have been unwrapped and rewrapped." She moved toward the tree. "Look here. You can see where the cellophane has been torn."

"Hmmm," Clive said, following her and examining the gift she held. He picked up another and turned it over.

"I also spoke with Charlotte, and she confirms that she did lose a necklace—a gold pendant with a cross on the front and a spade on the back in some sort of family crest—and that she did come back in to look for it."

"Perhaps she opened them all looking for the necklace?"

"I thought of that and asked her. She says she didn't."

"Maybe she's lying."

"I doubt it. She wouldn't have had time."

"I feel like I've seen something like this pendant she's describing," Clive mused, setting the gift he was holding back under the tree. "I just can't place it."

"She also cannot confirm that Noland locked the room after her. She was in too much of a hurry to notice."

"Speaking of Noland, I've found out that he was *not* fired by Cummings."

"I thought as much. Were you able to talk to any of the other staff members?"

"Just some of the cooks. Didn't get much out of them. Only one says he saw someone out back the night the gifts were taken, just as they were closing up."

"Could he identify him? Was it Noland?" she asked eagerly.

"No, it was the junior steward, apparently."

"Oh."

"Well, it's *still* odd. Why would he be standing out in the freezing cold? He had to have been standing there for a reason."

"Such as . . . ?"

"Maybe he knew the storage closet was unlocked and was waiting for his chance to go back in? Maybe he was working with someone? Noland maybe? Or maybe he was working alone and had stolen Cummings's or Noland's keys and was waiting for everyone to leave?"

"Or maybe he was waiting for one of the waitresses to get off so they could go have a drink."

"You know, you're awfully contrary."

"It's called 'playing devil's advocate.'" She tapped his nose with her finger. "And I learned it from *you.*"

Clive grinned. "You'll make a fine detective one day, you know."

Henrietta gasped. "*One day*? I'm a fine detective now! It was *me* that solved our last case, remember. Without any help from you, I might add!"

"I'm teasing, darling. You're first-rate. So much so that you can dictate our next step." He crossed his arms again.

"Don't patronize me, Inspector."

He suddenly pulled her to him and kissed her.

"Clive!" she sputtered when he finally released her. She quickly looked around the room, hoping no one had noticed.

"You naughty thing! Come on, let's go find this junior steward. What's his name, anyway?"

"Kip Kontzen, I believe."

"Kip Kontzen? That's an interesting name. All right, Mr. Kontzen." Henrietta slipped her arm through Clive's. "Where are you, and what can you tell us?"

CHAPTER 9

Elsie was tempted to slip her arm around Mr. Ferguson's, as the wind had severely picked up and threatened, she feared, to blow him completely over, but she didn't dare lose her grasp on Tom. She had resorted to tucking the poor cat into her coat, but she still needed both hands to keep him secure.

"Is it much farther, Mr. Ferguson?" she shouted through the wind.

Whether he heard her or not, Elsie wasn't sure, but he continued, nonetheless, to shuffle down the street, his body already bent, never mind the wind. Elsie, her eyes tearing from the cold, was beginning to regret her decision to follow this stranger out into the dark night. Perhaps he really had no home at all, she worried. Elsie followed him a bit further, wondering what to do, and was just about to call off the mission when he finally turned off Palmer onto Spalding. She felt a renewed tendril of hope that they might be headed for an actual destination after all, and that they were not aimlessly wandering. Elsie hoped it was near. Hadn't he said he lived not far off the Square?

"Mr. Ferguson," she called again. "Is this your street?"

The old man again didn't answer but continued his slow shuffling. Finally, blessedly, he stopped in front of a three-flat at the very end of Spalding before it crossed Dickens. It was the corner building, shabby and exposed, and litter had blown and was clinging to the foundation. Mr. Ferguson approached the front steps, and Elsie wondered how he was going to make it up all those crumbling cement stairs, but he instead turned to the right and pushed open a rusted iron gate beneath. Gripping the thin iron railing—loose in some places—with one gnarled hand, he began to hobble down. He took each step slowly, one by one, until he reached the bottom. He pushed open the rotting door of the garden apartment and disappeared inside without so much as a backward glance at her.

Elsie paused and looked up and down the street. At this hour and in the cold, no one else was out . . . no one who might hear her cry for help if she needed it. She felt she should follow Mr. Ferguson into the dark apartment, but a warning bell was sounding. Her right leg began to shake a little. Ever since she had followed her old flame, Harrison Barnes-Smith, into his house and had then been subjected to his . . . his . . . advances, she was overly cautious now.

"Mr. Ferguson?" she called, pushing the gate open a little, as it had swung back with a screech after the old man had passed through. The front door remained open, however, but no light had been switched on. Only blackness spilled out. Where was this Irene he had mentioned wanting to get home to? Was she out? And why didn't he switch on a light?

"Mr. Ferguson?" Elsie called again and wondered if maybe he had fallen over. At that moment, Tom jumped from her arms and bounded down the cement steps and into the apartment.

Elsie hesitated, wondering what to do. She had seen Mr. Ferguson and Tom home; wasn't that enough? But the door remained open; what if Tom escaped again? Elsie pushed her way through the gate and descended two steps. "Mr. Ferguson?" she called. Tentatively, she descended a few more. She waited a moment and, hearing nothing, crept down the rest. She stood in front of the door and peered into the dark interior. She supposed she should go in and check; after all, he was a crippled old man—it's not as if he could overpower her, not like Harrison . . .

Her heart pounding, Elsie tentatively stepped inside, surprised by how cold it was. A strong smell of cat urine hit her. "Mr. Ferguson, are you all right?" she called, feeling her way in the darkness. She could see a flicker of light ahead and moved toward it. She crept down a short hallway into what she guessed was probably the kitchen and nearly jumped when she saw Mr. Ferguson, illuminated by candlelight, holding another cat while Tom, meowing, rubbed his body against the man's legs.

"Say hello, Irene," Mr. Ferguson said, holding the cat up for Elsie to see.

Irene? *Irene was a cat?*

Quickly, Elsie began to piece together the story in front of her. She looked around the shabby kitchen, noting the piled dishes and stacks of old newspapers, empty tin cans, and old milk jugs. Even some dry, crumpled leaves that had blown from an opening somewhere. Oh, this poor man! "Mr. Ferguson, do you live here alone?"

"No, I've got Tom and Irene here."

"But it's so cold . . ."

"Aye, they turned the heat off after Molly died." He continued to pet the purring Irene.

"Was . . . was Molly another cat?" Elsie asked hesitantly.

Mr. Ferguson's head shot up. "Molly was me wife."

"Oh, I'm terribly sorry. How long has she been gone?" Elsie looked around the dark room again, trying to guess.

"'Bout four years, I reckon."

Elsie bit her lip, wondering how this poor man had survived in this hovel alone with just his cats, especially during Chicago's frigid winters. Mr. Ferguson sat down heavily in a nearby kitchen chair, still holding on to Irene. Elsie waited for him to do or say something, but he seemed to have nothing to do but sit there and pet his cats. Tom, meanwhile, jumped up on the counter and began licking the remains of whatever was on the top plate of a precarious stack.

Elsie wasn't sure what to do. She couldn't just leave him here! "Mr. Ferguson, I know it's late, but why don't you come back with me and spend the night? You can bring Tom and Irene, too. The children would love it," she tried to say as convincingly as she could. She would worry about Gunther's allergies later.

Mr. Ferguson did not look up but continued to pet Irene. "Nah. Thanks just the same. But Irene and Tom is never been away from home fer the night. Reckon they'd be addled. An' I promised Molly I'd look after 'em, so that's what I'm doin'." He looked up at Elsie now.

"Well," she faltered. "It might be nice for them to have a change. 'Specially at Christmas. Don't you think? A nice warm bed, perhaps a bath, a big bowl of food?"

Not a muscle of Mr. Ferguson's face moved, but Elsie could tell by its very immobility that he was considering it.

"And the same for you, of course," she added gently. "Chef's made a lovely pork roast for tonight, with potatoes and beans. A banana crème pie for dessert. Perhaps a drop of whiskey after?"

"Well." Mr. Ferguson shifted. "Well. I don't rightly know if I should. Maybe Molly wouldn't like it if I left. I told her I wouldn't, ya see. Told her I'd look after 'em."

Elsie cleared her throat. She had a long history of coaxing strays. She knew she had to proceed cautiously. "I don't think Molly would mind if you left for just a night," she said gently. "She'd be happy for Tom and Irene—and you—to have a little visit with us. I think she'd want you to."

"I don' know." He looked around forlornly.

"Tell you what," she said cheerfully. "Let's go back. We'll have dinner, and if you don't want to stay the night, my husband will run you back in the car. How does that sound?"

"Well . . ."

Elsie remained very still, trying to control her shivering.

"Roast pork, ya say? And whiskey?"

Elsie bit her lip. Perhaps she shouldn't have mentioned the whiskey . . . but it was too late now. "Yes. Chef does a lovely roast. Fluffy mashed potatoes, lots of butter."

Mr. Ferguson's lips shifted. "Well . . . guess we could go fer one night, eh, Irene? What you say, Tom?" he said, twisting as best he could to see the cat languidly lying on the counter now, his tail swishing. "But how we gonna get 'em there? Don't think I can carry 'em all that way."

"Not to worry! I have six younger brothers and sisters; I'm used to holding one or more of them at any given time. I can surely carry both Tom and Irene. I'll put them in my coat all cozy, like, so they won't be cold. Here, let me help you." She slowly approached Mr. Ferguson and took Irene from his arms and then, shifting her, was able to grab hold of Mr. Ferguson and help get him up. "That's it. Now, you come here, Tom. Let's get you sorted." Elsie picked up the docile Tom, but when she tried to tuck them inside her coat, it was impossible to hold them both, and they jumped out. Mr. Ferguson didn't seem aware of the dilemma and was blowing his nose in a handkerchief he had produced from somewhere.

Elsie looked around the room and spotted a wooden milk crate. If she could corral them in the crate, she reasoned, she could throw a blanket or a sweater or a coat over the top to prevent them jumping out. Tom was prowling around Mr. Ferguson's legs, who looked down at him for a moment and then went back to blowing his nose.

Elsie was able to easily catch Tom and gently put him in the crate, which she shifted now to her hip. Irene, perhaps sensing something was up, jumped on top of the counter.

"Mr. Ferguson, why don't you get Irene? She seems a little skittish."

Mr. Ferguson seemed to snap back into the present moment and stuffed his handkerchief in his coat pocket. "What? Oh. Irene? Irene," he said, turning toward the counter where Elsie had nodded, "come here, lassie. There you be, I've got ya now."

"Here, put her in here," Elsie said, holding out the crate. "I'm going to carry them this way."

"Oh, aye. That'd be good." Mr. Ferguson plopped the cat into the crate. "Now, you behave, missy. We're goin' out." Mr. Ferguson stiffened then and looked around. "Oh, I don' know.

Maybe we should just stay here." Elsie could see the fright in his eyes, and she felt a wave of pity.

"It'll be okay, Mr. Ferguson," she said gently. "We'll have a lovely evening together. Tom and Irene will have a splendid time. Molly would want them to, don't you think?"

Mr. Ferguson's cloudy eyes stared at the wall beyond, and then he gave a little nod. Having apparently decided, he gripped his cane and began shuffling across the room. Elsie took this as her cue and led the way toward the front door. Now that her eyes were accustomed to the dark, she could more easily navigate. When she got to the door, she noticed that the bottom was warped and that it didn't entirely close properly, which didn't help keeping out the frigid air.

She passed through first, Mr. Ferguson hobbling along after her. He pulled the door closed as tightly as he could, and then turned to begin what was probably a painful climb up the steps. Elsie opened her mouth to ask if he wanted to lock the door, but then thought better of it, remembering that it hadn't been locked when they came in. And what difference would it make? There was nothing there to steal.

"Come on," she said, gently helping him with one hand while she balanced the crate against her hip. "Let's get you home."

CHAPTER 10

Henrietta wondered how much longer it would be before they could go home. It was getting late, and she was worried about Teddy. They had attempted to track down the junior steward, Kip Kontzen, who had been seen loitering out back after hours on the night the gifts were stolen, but he was proving difficult to find.

Finally, they had decided to seek out Mr. Cummings. Failing to find him in his office, however, Clive and Henrietta had made their way to the club's kitchen, where Henrietta had predicted he might be on the night of such a big event—barking orders, directing staff, and mitigating small disasters.

Tentatively, they had pushed through the swinging doors and, leaving behind the elegant, festive atmosphere of the club, stepped into a frantic vortex of noise and chaos. Dozens of staff members were flying around prepping food, cooking, scraping, washing, and dropping off. Cooks shouted to each other in Italian. No one even noticed the presence of the two strangers.

Henrietta's eyes quickly darted around the room and alighted on Mr. Cummings himself, talking on a telephone mounted on the white-tiled wall of the club's kitchen. He looked extremely out of place in his tuxedo and old-fashioned spats next to the cooks frantically turning meat on a grill and carrying huge pots of water, their aprons stained with almost every shade of food.

"I said *by tomorrow*!" Mr. Cummings shouted into the receiver and banged it down. He pulled out a handkerchief from his breast pocket and began hurriedly mopping his dripping forehead. He turned and, upon catching sight of Clive and Henrietta standing just inside the doors, his eyes bulged dangerously and his cheeks flushed.

"What is it, Mr. Howard?" he exclaimed, waddling toward them. "Dear God, what's happened now?"

"Can we speak with you outside, Mr. Cummings?" Henrietta shouted over the din. "It's awfully noisy in here. And I daresay a bit warm." Indeed, it was so hot in the kitchen that Henrietta feared her makeup would soon begin to melt if they remained any longer.

Without answering, Mr. Cummings barged through the swinging doors, looking around worriedly, as if expecting a fire or some other such calamity. "Has something gone wrong in the ballroom?" he asked, abruptly halting just outside the kitchen and turning to them. "Why was I not informed?"

"No, nothing's wrong, Mr. Cummings," Henrietta answered. "We're just looking for one of your stewards. Kip Kontzen? Might we have a word with him?"

Mr. Cummings stared at them, as if he didn't comprehend. "Now?" he finally asked, incredulous.

"It will just take a moment. We're still investigating the missing gifts."

"Gifts? Did they go missing again?" He turned and began walking swiftly down the hall, as if to inspect the tree himself.

"No, Mr. Cummings!" Henrietta called. "They're all still there!"

The poor manager halted, turned, and trudged back toward them, mopping his brow again. "Well, why didn't you say that in the first place? If they're not missing, then what's the problem?"

Clive pinched the bridge of his nose. "We're still trying to ascertain who took them in the first place and why."

Mr. Cummings rolled his eyes and shrugged. "Well, suit yourself, like, Mr. Howard." He let out an exhausted breath. "But I shouldn't worry about that. Why don't you and your lovely wife go off and enjoy the dancing?" He tried to smile convincingly, as if Clive and Henrietta were children to be amused. "As you can imagine, I am a bit busy at the moment."

"We will, Mr. Cummings, but first we'd like a word with Mr. Kontzen. If he can be spared, that is."

Mr. Cummings twisted his lips from side to side. "All right. But just for a moment. I've got him out helping the valets tonight. They're short two men."

Mr. Cummings led the way to his office, which, Henrietta noticed, was not locked. Mr. Cummings switched on the light and marched to his desk. He picked up the telephone and dialed a number. He waited a moment and then barked, "Tell Kontzen to report to my office immediately. Yes, now. That's what *immediately* means!" He banged the phone down. "Can't get the help these days," he said disgustedly. He moved around to the other side of the desk and yanked open the top right-hand drawer. "Cigar?"

"No, thanks," Clive said. "Seeing as you're in a hurry."

"I'm always in a hurry, Mr. Howard. Doesn't stop me from smoking a cigar." He threw himself heavily into his swivel chair. "What do you want with Kontzen, anyway?" He picked up the half-smoked cigar in an ashtray near his elbow and tried puffing it, but it was cold. "You don't suspect him of being messed up in this prank, do you? Couldn't be him."

"How can you be so sure?" Clive's eyes narrowed.

"I just am. I have a knack for knowing these things. I know my staff, and it wasn't him." He picked out a match from an open box and struck it roughly along the side. It burst into flame.

"Well, who *do* you think it was, then?"

"That I can't say. Don't think it was *any* of my staff, actually." He held the match to the cold cigar gripped between his teeth.

"What about Noland Peters?" Clive asked.

Henrietta noticed that Cummings's right cheek rippled slightly, but he shook his head. "Nah. Not him, either." He puffed deeply. "He's an arrogant little chiver, but he's not a thief. He's had plenty a chances to steal in the past, but didn't. Barking up the wrong tree there, to put it proverbially, Mr. Howard. Like they say on the radio shows."

There was a knock on the door then, and the young man Henrietta recognized as having been Noland's assistant the other day entered. He gave Clive and Henrietta a quick nervous glance, but he fixed his gaze on his boss.

"Yes, Mr. Cummings?" he squeaked.

"Mr. and Mrs. Howard wish a word with you. And your answers better be true, boy," Mr. Cummings mumbled as he blew out a cloud of smoke.

"Yes, Mr. Cummings." He gave Clive and Henrietta another sideways glance and then looked at the floor.

"Look, kid, we'll be fast." Clive crossed his arms. "What do you know about the gifts that went missing?"

Kip looked up at him. "Nothing, Mr. Howard! Honest!"

"Then why were you loitering around the back that night after closing?"

Kip's eyes darted nervously to Mr. Cummings, who was now puffing like a chimney. "I . . . I wasn't!"

"Cut the crap, kid. Someone saw you, so spill it."

"Who?"

"It doesn't matter. Just answer the question."

"I . . . I was waiting for someone."

"Who? Noland Peters?"

"Noland?" He looked baffled.

"The two of you waited for everyone to leave and then went back in and stole the gifts, right? Admit it."

Mr. Cummings lowered his cigar, eyeing Kip carefully.

"No! That's not true!" Kip squeaked again. "I have no idea who took the gifts!"

Henrietta put a hand on Clive's arm. "Okay, Kip," she said gently. "Why were you out there? Can anyone vouch for you?"

Kip shot another wary glance at Mr. Cummings and then hung his head. "I was waiting for Luella."

"Who's Luella?" Clive asked.

"She's one of the waitresses. I . . . I had a Christmas present for her, and I didn't get a chance all night to give it to her. In private. So I waited out back for her to come out."

"Did she?"

"Eventually, yes. I was nearly frozen to death by then."

"Then what?"

"Nothing! I said good night and we parted ways."

"Well, why didn't you just say so in the first place?"

"Because," Mr. Cummings interjected, removing his cigar from his mouth now, "fraternization among the staff is strictly forbidden."

Henrietta was about to comment that that was a silly rule, but Mr. Cummings spoke first. "Satisfied?" he asked Clive. "I'll deal with you later, Mr. Kontzen. Get back to work."

Kip immediately moved toward the door, but Clive put a hand on his upper arm and stopped him.

"Wait. Did you see anything or anyone else out there? Anything unusual?"

Kip's eyes looked momentarily at Mr. Cummings before quickly answering. "No. Nothing. Excuse me, sir," he said, and hurried from the room.

Mr. Cummings stood. "Now, if you don't mind. I need to check the champagne stores. Seems we're running a bit lower than expected." He ushered them to the door.

"Oh?" Clive asked as the manager held open the door now. "Is that unusual?"

"Mr. Howard, please! For the love of God. Not everything's a mystery! Some of us have actual work to do. Please!" He gestured toward the hallway.

Henrietta could tell Clive was about to angrily retort, so she looped her arm through his and led him out of the room. "Come along, darling. They're playing our song."

Cummings closed the door loudly behind them. It wasn't an actual slam, but nearly.

"Well, there goes that theory," Henrietta said. "I guess it wasn't Kip Kontzen."

"He's lying about something. I think he's covering for Peters. And Cummings is acting a little suspicious, too." Clive angrily rubbed his free hand through his hair.

"Agreed. But I don't know how much more we're going to be able to uncover tonight, if ever, considering the gifts are going to be delivered tomorrow."

"Unless we stop them."

"Well, it's Victoria Braithewaite you would have to convince, and I don't think that's a realistic option. And since we're not acting in an official police capacity, I don't think we have the power to overrule her. No one else seems to care about who took them and why, so I don't think we have any choice but to let it go, too, darling." Henrietta brushed the back of her fingers against his cheek.

Clive let out a deep, irritated breath. "I suppose you're right, but I can just feel the solution is nearly within our grasp."

"You were probably right the first time. It was probably just a silly prank."

"All the more reason why I want to figure this out."

"It's Christmas, Inspector," she said seductively, straightening his white bow tie. "Let's try to forget it."

Clive closed his eyes resignedly. "All right. But I—"

"Clive! There you are!" exclaimed Antonia. "I've been looking everywhere for the two of you. Why have you abandoned the ball? I was afraid you might have already left. Come back in!" she insisted.

With a heavy sigh, Clive followed, and Lord and Lady Linley dutifully spent the rest of the evening dancing with what seemed a large percentage of the crowd without any more chances of breaking away. Henrietta hoped to perhaps have one more conversation with Charlotte, but, alas, she did not get the chance. She once caught sight of her chatting with Beatrice, and another time she saw her on the dance floor with none other than Mr. Braithewaite, who thankfully seemed to have forgotten his promised second dance with Henrietta.

Beatrice, she noticed, had not been asked to dance at all. Henrietta then implored Clive to go ask her, which he had gallantly done, but the girl had surprisingly declined! Perhaps she was nervous? Shy? A poor dancer? Either way, Henrietta felt sorry for her, especially next to the beautiful and charming Charlotte.

Finally, well past midnight, Henrietta whispered to Clive that perhaps they might leave, as she was anxious to get back to Teddy, though it would never do to use that excuse with Antonia. She would have to invent one. The ballroom was thinning out now, but they did not see Antonia—or Sidney, for that matter. They finally located her in one of the small sitting rooms off the ballroom, where she was seated with several of her cronies, Victoria Braithewaite, however, *not* being one of them.

"I have a terrible headache, I'm afraid, Antonia," Henrietta fibbed, after Clive informed her that they were going home.

"A headache! Oh, I hope you're not ill!" Antonia chirped worriedly. "Perhaps we should telephone Dr. Ferrington."

"No, I'm perfectly fine, I assure you," Henrietta said quickly. "Just fatigued."

"Well, of course you would be. Getting up all hours of the night with that baby. That's what she does, you know," she said to the woman on her right. "Unnatural, I say."

The woman next to her, Mrs. Wilcox, screwed up her face in surprise.

"And then she insisted on Christmas shopping yesterday! In this cold. It's no wonder you're ill!" Antonia said with more annoyance than perhaps she really meant.

"Mrs. Patterson, Mrs. Wilcox, I bid you good evening," Clive said politely. "Mother." He gave Antonia a deferential nod and then led Henrietta toward the foyer.

"Where's Sidney?" Henrietta asked, gazing around the ballroom again as they wound their way along the edges.

"I haven't seen much of him at all tonight. He's probably in the men's lounge playing billiards. Or maybe he's sulking somewhere."

"That's very ungenerous, Clive. I thought you made up with him."

"I did! But he still seems to be avoiding me. I can only apologize so many times, you know."

"Well, what happened when you went to inspect the stables? You never said."

"It was all very civil."

They had reached the foyer now, and they were surprised when Kip Kontzen stepped forward to take their ticket.

"You still here?" Clive asked.

Kip nodded nervously. "Yes, sir," he said, scurrying to the direction of the cloak room. Within minutes he returned carrying Henrietta's stole and Clive's top hat.

Clive had meanwhile opened his wallet and pulled out a twenty-dollar bill. He held it up between his second and third finger. Kip eyed it hungrily. Clive crumpled the bill then and stuffed it in Kip's jacket pocket. Kip stared at it and then looked back at Clive.

"Suppose you tell us what else you saw that night."

Kip looked around, his brow knit. "I . . . I don't know."

"You sure you didn't see any strange cars or trucks drive up while you were waiting for this Luella? Think, man."

Kip, though he was hardly a man, thought for a moment. "Not that I can remember. Nothing 'cept Mr. Braithewaite's car. But that's not unusual." He shrugged.

"What do you mean 'it's not unusual'?"

Kip's face blanched.

"Out with it!"

"Well," Kip squeaked, "Mr. Braithewaite is in the habit of coming back after hours to . . . to . . . well, he does like the waitresses, sir. He . . . he comes back sometimes and picks one of them up."

"What a wretch!" Clive exclaimed.

"Did you see Noland at all?" Henrietta pulled her stole tighter, suddenly chilled.

Kip looked nervously from one to the other.

"Well, did you?" Clive demanded.

"Just for a minute," he squeaked again. "He came out and spoke to the driver and then . . ."

"And then?"

"Well, then Luella came out, and I was distracted by her. I didn't see what else happened."

"Damn it," Clive muttered.

"Should I . . . should I go fetch your car now, sir?"

"What? Yes," Clive said with a sigh. "Yes, I suppose so."

Noland hurried to the wooden box near the door and removed the keys to the Alfa and then scurried toward the door.

"Just one more question, Kontzen," Clive called.

Kip halted and turned slowly back around. "Yes, sir?"

"Does Mr. Cummings know about Braithewaite's clandestine visits?"

"I should think so, sir. Mr. Cummings knows everything."

"And what about Noland? How does he fit into all of this?"

"That's easy, sir. Mr. Peters is Mr. Cummings's nephew."

CHAPTER 11

"Are you ready to meet Uncle Glenn and Aunt Julia?" Henrietta babbled to Teddy, who was sitting brightly on her lap and dressed in a pale-blue velvet sailor suit romper, which matched his eyes perfectly. Henrietta wrapped her finger around a lock of hair atop his head, trying to solidify the curl that was there.

She was eager to show him off to Julia, who was like another sister to her, but more than that, she wanted to see for herself if Julia was happy in her new life away from the North Shore gilded set and her brutish former husband, Randolph, under whose hand she had suffered greatly.

Henrietta had written many tender letters to Julia while her sister-in-law recuperated at Highbury and had thoroughly rejoiced when Julia wrote back with the news that she was marrying Glenn Forbes, Sidney's nephew, who had arrived at Highbury to purchase one of Alcott's paintings, *El Rio de*

Luz. Antonia had refused at the time to sell it to him, but he had absconded with something even more precious before he returned to Texas, namely Julia's wounded heart. It had been Henrietta's idea to send them *El Rio* as a wedding gift, to which Clive had agreed. The newlyweds had apparently been overjoyed with the gift, particularly, of course, Glenn.

"You sure you're going to be okay?" Edna said, folding up Teddy's blanket. "Maybe we should stay the night."

"Edna! We've discussed this. I insist that you and Pascal have Christmas Eve *and* Christmas Day off. It's only fair. And I'm sure you're anxious to introduce your new husband to your mother."

Edna broke into a smile. "Well, they *are* all anxious, I must admit, miss. And Pascal's quite looking forward to experiencing an American Christmas, seeing how he's so enamored of the United States. He's been to the pictures six times already!"

"Six times!"

"Well, he does fancy American films. And Mr. Clive, as you know, don't have much for him to do. 'Specially here." Edna adjusted the fold of Teddy's collar. "Pascal offered to serve as a footman or even to work in the stables, such as they are, but Mr. Clive wouldn't hear of it. 'It'll only upset Billings,' is what he said to him and instead gives him the afternoons off."

"How generous," Henrietta said with raised eyebrows, thinking about how much Clive had changed. "I'm sorry I haven't done the same."

"Nonsense! I've plenty to do, as you know. And I wouldn't like to spend so much time away from the mister. You're more like my family than my own, I reckon, miss," she said a little wistfully.

"I feel the same, Edna. Truly." She reached out a hand, and Edna, shifting the blanket in her arms, squeezed it. "But what about Pascal? Doesn't he miss *his* family?"

Edna shrugged. "Not much. He don't have much family left back in Strasbourg. Just a brother and a great aunt, I think." She laid the blanket at the end of the bed. "But he's been trying to teach me some French Christmas customs. Strange they are over there. Worse than the English."

Henrietta laughed. "Well, enjoy yourself. You deserve it!"

"But what about little mister?" Edna held out her finger to him, and he wrapped his chubby fist around it. "Don't know what I'll do without him. And what about you, miss? Late nights with Christmas, an' all?"

"Of course, I'll be all right. It'll just give me an excuse to retire early." She tried to sound confident, but in truth, she *was* a tad worried about how she would fare, as she hadn't been completely alone with Teddy since Edna and Pascal had left for their honeymoon in Paris. Somehow, though, she had managed to do it then, and she would again, she resolved. After all, Teddy was several months older now and given to sleeping through the night—most nights, anyway. "And if I'm in a jam downstairs, I'll just have to leave him with Nanny Simms for a few hours."

"Oh, no, miss! Please don't do that! She's a sourpuss if ever I saw one. Poor Mr. Clive, having to endure that as a child. No wonder—"

"No wonder what?"

Edna's face turned red. "Nothing, miss."

Henrietta laughed out loud.

There was a knock on the door then, and Clive entered. "They're here!"

Henrietta's heart flipped a little as she stood, shifting Teddy onto her hip and smoothing his hair one more time.

"You want me to carry him down, miss?" Edna asked eagerly, hovering.

"No, I've got him. That'll be all for now, Edna."

"Well, if you're sure, like . . ."

Henrietta gave her a hurried, encouraging smile. "Yes, I'm sure. We'll be back up shortly, I imagine, and then you can take him for the evening."

"Very good, miss."

Henrietta joined Clive in the hallway, who himself seemed uncharacteristically excited, and together they walked down the gallery hallway to the landing above the grand black-and-white checkered foyer.

"There they are!" Julia called from below. The servants had already removed the guests' coats, and Julia stood at the foot of the stairs, smartly arrayed in a stylish tweed traveling suit. "Lord and lady of the manor! Though I do beg your pardon, Mother," she said over her shoulder at Antonia, who was standing nearby, "as it is still your house. And Sidney's, of course."

Henrietta couldn't help but smile. It was marvelous to see Julia so bright and fresh and . . . well . . . happy. She didn't think she had ever seen Julia looking so young, though she was in truth a year older than Clive.

Henrietta descended the grand staircase as quickly as she dared, Clive trailing. Julia met her at the bottom and gave her a kiss on both cheeks. "And this must be my nephew!" she exclaimed, looking at Teddy lovingly. "Hello, Teddy!" she cooed. "I've always wanted to be an auntie!"

Teddy promptly hid his face in Henrietta's neck. Julia laughed. "Randy was the same at that age, weren't you?" she said, putting her arm around the tall, slim boy who had sidled up to her. Henrietta was amazed at how much he had grown. He was nearly up to Julia's shoulder! But what was even more startling was how similar he looked to Randolph, Sr. It was uncanny, and it threw Henrietta off just a little. She smiled at him to hide her discomfort.

"Randy, is it?" she asked.

"Yes, that's what he prefers to be called now, don't you?" Julia asked him gently.

"And is Howard to be called Howie?" Henrietta asked, looking beyond Julia to where the younger of the boys stood, bravely allowing himself to be "lavished" with a prim kiss and an awkward hug from Antonia.

"Heavens, no!" Julia laughed. "He insists on Howard."

"He's grown, too."

"Clive, how the hell are you?" Glenn said, coming up and holding out a hand. Clive shook it firmly. "How's London? We'll have to talk later. Got a business idea I want to run by you and Uncle Sid."

"I look forward to it." Clive tilted his head slightly. "How was the drive up?"

"Not bad. Glad we made it before the snow."

"Is it really gonna snow, Pops?" Howard asked, pulling on his pant leg.

Henrietta caught the address and thought it fitting. The boys couldn't exactly call Glenn "Father" or "Dad," seeing as Randolph was unfortunately still alive and well. Henrietta wondered if Randolph would try to see the boys while they were here. Probably not, as Julia had told her via letters that once the divorce had been finalized, Randolph had ceased all contact. Though no words had been spoken to the effect, Henrietta had a hunch that Sidney and Clive had privately threatened him from ever contacting Julia or the boys again. That and the money they had given to pay off his gambling debts had probably convinced him.

Henrietta watched Howard. Though he was perfectly behaved, she could tell he had a rambunctious spirit just from the way he stood in front of Antonia. He was more stout than his brother and more ruddy, and if Henrietta didn't know better, he could easily pass for Glenn's natural son.

He ran over now to Julia. "Can I hold the baby?" he asked, slightly hanging on her arm.

"Maybe later," Julia said, tousling his hair. "He's shy just at the moment. Let him get used to us."

"Can he walk?" Howard asked Henrietta.

"Not just yet." She gave him a smile. "He's just learning to crawl. Maybe his two cousins could help him."

"Yeah, okay," Howard said. "We're gonna teach our baby, too, ain't we, Randy?"

"Baby?" Henrietta looked curiously at Julia.

Julia laughed. "Howard! That was supposed to be a surprise." She laughed again and took Glenn's hand. "Yes," she said, her hand going to her stomach as she turned to include her mother in the announcement, "we're having a baby!"

"Oh, Julia!" exclaimed Henrietta. "That's wonderful! Oh, I'm so happy for you."

"Yes, what a surprise!" Antonia said, coming closer. By her tone, Henrietta wasn't sure if she was pleased or disappointed. "It seems so soon, Julia."

"Congratulations, Glenn." Clive clapped him on the back.

"We're hoping for a girl, aren't we?" Julia turned to look at Glenn, who answered with a nod.

"We sure are," Glenn said, tousling Howard's hair again. "These two hooligans could use a sister."

"It seems a celebration is in order," Sidney said, joining the little group now. "I'll have Billings bring some champagne once you're settled."

"Come on, Randy. Race you upstairs!" Howard called and bolted toward the grand staircase. Randy, after giving Julia a little look for approval, hurried after him.

"Boys! Young gentlemen do *not* run!" Antonia called after them. The boys dutifully slowed until they had rounded the curve in the stairs, and then returned to a healthy trot once they were out of sight. "Do you allow them to run in the house at home, Julia?" Antonia chided. "It's most unseemly."

"It's a different life at the ranch, Antonia," Glenn said with an easy smile.

He was very winsome with his good looks and easy charm, but Antonia screwed up her face nonetheless. "Yes, I imagine it is," she said stiffly. "But Julia, you aren't really planning on having the baby in Texas, are you?"

Julia gave a little laugh. "Of course I am, Mother. It isn't the wilds of Africa, you know." She put an arm around her mother's shoulders. "The house looks beautiful, Mother. Even more so than I remember."

Antonia's tight face relaxed into a crooked grin as she looked around at the Christmas decorations. "Yes, well, the servants did it all, of course."

"Still," Julia slipped an arm through her mother's. "It's lovely. Let's sit down, and you can tell me all about the ball," she said, leading her toward the drawing room.

Antonia pulled back in alarm. "But don't you wish to change?" She looked her daughter up and down as if searching for bits of dirt. "Freshen up? The train is so awfully dirty."

"First class is immaculate, Mother, as you well know. We'll change before dinner. Let's talk a bit first. I want to know everything!"

A fire was already going in the drawing room when they entered, and the ornaments on the tree in the corner sparkled in reflection. Albert scurried around the room, turning on lamps. Julia took a place on the edge of the sofa, and Henrietta sat beside her, Teddy in her lap. Julia immediately began to make silly faces at him to get him to smile, and miraculously, after only a few attempts, he rewarded her with one.

"Henrietta, would he not be more comfortable upstairs in the nursery?" Antonia's voice was strained as she eyed Teddy disapprovingly.

"Perhaps, but Edna is busy packing."

"Packing? Whatever for?" Antonia's face was one of alarm.

"We've given her and Pascal the next two days off to spend Christmas with Edna's family. They only live down in Evanston."

"The next two days! Are you mad? I can't imagine how you'll cope. And what about tomorrow in Palmer Square? You can't possibly think of going without a maid or a nanny. I don't see what you have against Nanny Simms." Antonia frowned and looked at Julia, perhaps hoping for encouragement. "It was unheard of in my day for a child to be seen below after four in the afternoon."

"If he fusses, we will remove him from the room, Mother," Clive said sternly.

"But then Henrietta will have to leave, too. You must see how silly this is."

"So how was the ball, Mother?" Julia asked, turning her attention to her. "You did say you'd tell us." She continued to look steadily at her mother, like an attentive schoolgirl, with only one recalcitrant sideways glance at Teddy, during which she quickly stuck out her tongue at him. He smiled again.

"It went off splendidly I think, don't you, Henrietta?"

"Yes, it was marvelous, Antonia. Perfect, in fact."

"All except Victoria." Antonia drew herself up with a sniff. "She was really rather vexing."

"Up to her old tricks, was she?" Julia pursed her lips at Teddy in imitation of a goldfish, and Teddy actually laughed. Henrietta shot a surprised look at Clive, who returned it with a grin.

"Well, that's one way of putting it," Antonia lamented. "But she seems to be getting worse."

"Perhaps she was just upset about the stolen gifts," Sidney suggested from his perch near the fireplace. He clasped his hands behind his back.

"What's this?" Julia finally pulled her gaze from Teddy and turned her attention back to her mother. "Stolen gifts?"

Antonia let out a sigh. "Yes, someone stole the gifts for the poor a few nights ago, but then they brought them back. Seemingly untouched. Obviously a prank."

"Oooh! How perfectly delicious," Julia cooed. "A case! What a splendid Christmas gift for you, Clive. Perhaps some-one orchestrated it for that very reason." She raised an eyebrow questioningly at Henrietta and then smiled. "Have you solved it?" Julia asked her brother.

Clive crossed his legs and casually leaned his head on his fist, his arm propped up on the side of the wingback chair he was reclining in. "Not yet. But I'm working on it."

"Working on it?" Antonia exclaimed. "But why? The gifts are being delivered tomorrow! Clive, must you slouch?"

Clive remained as he was.

"Any suspects?" Glenn asked.

"Oooh, yes! Do tell! This is like listening to a radio program. I always wanted to be a lady detective! I've quite envied you in that respect, Henrietta." She held out her hands to Teddy, who, after a few moments of hesitation, leaned toward her. Gently, Julia eased him onto her lap and let him pull at her necklace.

"Well, I'm afraid we don't have much time for that anymore," Henrietta said, watching Teddy carefully, amazed that he had gone to a stranger. "We're much too busy in London."

"Busy with all of the swells?" Julia shot Clive a mischievous grin. "How *do* you like being Lord Linley, Clive? You never wanted anything to do with Highbury, much less a crumbling castle in the English countryside. Must be absolute *torture* for you."

"It has its advantages," Clive said, standing now and walking toward the drinks cart. He lifted the heavy stopper from a thick crystal bottle and poured a cognac. "Anyone else?"

"Billings should be here any minute with the champagne," Sidney offered.

Clive ignored him.

"I'll have one." Glenn stood up and wandered over. "So," he said, taking the glass Clive offered, "*do* you miss detecting?"

Clive took a long drink. "I hardly think of it."

"I can't believe that!" Julia chimed from across the room. "Now, do tell us all the details of the Case of the Missing Christmas Gifts without any more interruption! We're all in suspense." She gave Teddy a little kiss on the head.

Clive nodded his head at Henrietta, inviting her to elaborate.

"Well, there's nothing much to tell," she faltered and explained as much as they knew, deciding at the last minute to leave out the part about Hugh Braithewaite's clandestine visits after hours to pick up waitresses.

"So, there's the steward, the junior steward, Mr. Cummings, Luella the waitress, and the young woman who lost her necklace," Julia rattled off. "What was her name again?"

"Charlotte MacKenzie," Henrietta answered.

"Ah, yes. I don't think I know her, do I, Mother?"

"No, she's from New York. The daughter of one of Victoria's childhood friends. Though I don't know why she flaunts it. The brother has quite ruined the family's reputation, if they even had one to begin with."

"Perhaps that was the reason for her being here. To get away from the scandal?" Julia reasoned. "Everyone deserves a second chance, you know." She said this last bit softly and looked lovingly across at Glenn. "Especially when it wasn't her fault to begin with."

"Be that as it may," Antonia said stiffly, missing the soft wink Glenn shot Julia across the room, "Charlotte has nothing to do with this, so I don't know why we're discussing her."

"My guess is that it's this Peters character in league with Cummings, especially given the familial connection," Glenn said, taking a long drink.

"I'm of that mind, too," Clive responded. "But I don't have any proof, and not much to go on. If I was given leave to search all the boxes, I might uncover some clue. But as it is, my hands are tied." He glared at Antonia.

"Oh, I don't know," Julia mused. "I think there's something to poor Charlotte's necklace. Was it valuable?"

"From the sound of it, no." Henrietta took a glass of the champagne from the silver tray Billings now offered, having somehow inconspicuously entered the room with a silver platter adorned with several glasses of bubbling champagne. "It was a pendant of sorts, apparently. On the front was a cross with a small diamond and on the back was a crest with a spade. And maybe corn or wheat, or something like that."

"That sounds oddly familiar." Julia mused.

"Funny. Clive said the same thing."

Julia thought for a moment and then looked over at Clive. "Didn't Father have something similar? I'm sure I've seen it before."

Clive's face brightened. "That's it!" He snapped his fingers. "I remember it now! Excuse me." He hurried from the room. He was gone several long minutes, during which time Julia continued to try to get Teddy to laugh. Antonia watched them, frowning.

Clive strode back into the room carrying a worn velvet-covered box, the lid of which he had pried open. "Here it is! It was in his study." He held it out for the group to see, and, sure enough, it held a pendant that looked exactly like the one Charlotte had described as missing. "It's the Order of St. Isidore."

"The Order of St. Isidore?" Julia queried.

"It's a fraternal club at Cambridge." Clive carefully lifted the pendant from the box and held it up. "Only members received them. Secret rituals and all of that."

"I can hardly believe that of Father."

"It's true, though," Sidney said, stepping forward to try to get a closer look at the pendant. "Alcott *was* a member of the Order of St. Isidore."

"So how would Charlotte MacKenzie get such a thing? Surely her brother didn't go to Cambridge?"

"Maybe he stole it?" Henrietta suggested.

"Perhaps." Clive rubbed his chin. "Or maybe *she* did."

"What? From whom?" Antonia queried.

"From Hugh Braithewaite. Wasn't he at Cambridge with Father?" Clive looked to Sidney, who nodded.

"Yes, he was, but I'm not sure if he was a part of this particular group. He could have been." Sidney said with a shrug. "It would be easy enough to find out."

"I still think it's the steward and the manager," Glenn said. "That makes the most sense. If this Charlotte told the steward she lost a necklace, maybe he and Cummings put two and two together and searched the boxes for it, hoping it was valuable enough to sell."

"Perhaps," Clive said slowly. "I *do* think they are hiding something. But I think a visit to the Braithewaites' is in order. I have a few questions for old Hugh." He set down his glass and straightened his tie. "You'll excuse me, Mother."

"What, *now*?" Antonia exclaimed. "But . . . but Julia and Glenn have just arrived, and tomorrow is Christmas Eve!"

"Yes, all the more reason to do it now before the gifts are delivered. And before the snow starts. I'm sure Julia and Glenn will go up soon anyway to get settled, so why not?"

"But it's already *started* to snow!" Antonia exclaimed, looking past the group to the front windows, where, indeed, large flakes were beginning to float down. "This is madness, Clive."

"I'll be back before dinner. Coming?" he asked Henrietta. His face was all seriousness, but she thought she detected the beginnings of a grin at the corner of his mouth. She desperately wanted to go, but how could she? Clive had been right the other day when he accused her of missing their detective work as much as he did, but she was loath to leave Teddy, especially as it would mean interrupting Edna. Nor was she about to bundle him up and bring him with them on a case.

"Off you go!" Julia said cheerfully. "I've got him." She gave Teddy another kiss on the head. He was still enthralled with her necklace and was banging it now against her chest.

"Are you sure?" Henrietta scooted forward on the sofa, studying Teddy and wondering if he would be okay with her.

"Yes, go on! He'll hardly notice you're gone. And if he does cry, I'll have the boys come entertain him."

"This is what comes of not employing the proper servants," Antonia grumbled. "The whole thing is ridiculous in the extreme."

"Come on, darling. He'll be fine," Clive urged.

"All right, then," Henrietta said somewhat reluctantly, as she stood up. "Let me just get my hat!"

CHAPTER 12

"Clive, slow down! It's slippery!"

Clive gently applied the brakes, and the Alfa slid slightly. "Sorry, darling. I'm just thinking."

"Yes, I can tell." She gripped the side door handle. "Maybe this *is* a bit mad, Clive," Henrietta said, unintentionally quoting Antonia. "Have you considered what you'll do if no one's home?"

Clive shifted the Alfa into a lower gear. "Where else would they be on the day before the day before Christmas?"

"Oh, I don't know . . . shopping?"

"Hugh Braithewaite, shopping? I seriously doubt he's anywhere but in his cozy study, a fat cigar in hand. If we have any luck, Charlotte will be home, too."

"You don't really think she took it from Hugh, do you? She doesn't seem the thieving sort."

"Not many thieves do, darling."

Henrietta thought for a moment. "You know, there might be another explanation."

"Such as?"

"That Hugh *gave* it to Charlotte."

Clive glanced at her. "Go on."

"Well, considering the fact that he seems to be a bit of a philanderer, perhaps he gave the pendant to her as a token of his . . . his affection, shall we say, as grotesque as that sounds, but then she lost it. In a panic, she tells him that she's misplaced it, possibly while wrapping the gifts, so he went back late that night to retrieve it, realized it was too big of a job to do then and there, removed all the gifts, searched them, and then returned them the next day?"

"Darling, I think you give him too much credit. He doesn't seem all that intelligent."

"Well, it's not a very intelligent plan, is it?"

Clive laughed.

"Wouldn't it be simply too ironic, if the gifts had been right under Victoria's nose the whole time?"

"Would she really not have noticed?" Clive asked, pulling into the long driveway of the Braithewaite mansion. "Though, given the size of this place," Clive peered through the windshield, "maybe she didn't."

"How singular, Clive," Hugh snorted once they were shown into what was in fact a cozy, wood-paneled study with a roaring fire in the small ornate fireplace. "I'm not in the habit of entertaining at this hour. Victoria, I'm sorry to say, is not at home. Christmas shopping or some such thing with the girls. You know how ladies are this time of year. No offense to you, of course, Mrs. Howard. May I offer you tea? A sherry, perhaps? Please, do sit down."

"A sherry would be lovely, Mr. Braithewaite." Henrietta took a seat on the leather sofa, Clive following.

"Oh, do call me Hugh," the older man said, his moustache curling up along with his lips. He walked to a sideboard and selected a tall, thin bottle from an assortment arranged on a silver tray and poured a tiny glass full of amber liquid. "You, Clive? Or something stronger?"

"Sherry is fine."

"Very good." He poured two more and handed them one each before lowering himself into a leather armchair. He took a sip from his own small glass and nodded in appreciation. "Ah, yes. A very good vintage. 1892 it is. I once had the luck of partaking of an even older vintage at the—"

"Excuse me, Mr. Braithewaite, but—"

"Hugh."

Clive let out an imperceptible sigh. "Hugh. But we have some questions about the missing gifts."

"Missing gifts?" Mr. Braithewaite seemed genuinely confused.

"From the club?" Clive raised his eyebrows.

"Ah. Yes. I see. What about them? Not really my purview. More Victoria's. Though I think it was all squared away, wasn't it? Found and all that."

"Where were you on the night the gifts went missing?"

Hugh blinked several times. "Me? Why, I was here. Why do you ask?"

"Are you sure?"

Hugh blinked again, trying to remember. "Quite sure."

Clive glanced at Henrietta, only one eyebrow raised now, and then turned his attention back. "Then why were you seen at the Winnetka Country Club after hours?"

Mr. Braithewaite's eyes widened. "At the club? There must be some mistake. Who told you this?"

"A staff member. It doesn't matter who. He says, in fact, that your car is frequently seen there after hours . . . just as the staff are leaving."

Mr. Braithewaite's thick, porous cheeks flushed. "Look here! I don't know what you're implying, but I rather don't like your tone." He glowered, his nostrils flaring, at Clive, who calmly returned the stare full on. "I was here, if you must know. A headache, as I seem to recall."

"Can anyone verify that?"

"Verify? You doubt my word as a gentleman?"

Clive continued to stare at him.

Hugh gestured awkwardly. "Any of the servants can verify that."

"But they would be inclined to say what you wanted them to say, wouldn't they?"

"See here, Clive. I was a friend to your father, and I'm indulging you for his sake, but this has really gone too far now. The gifts are back, are they not? This seems more than a trifle unnecessary. And why on earth would I want some tidbits wrapped up for the poor?"

"Because you were looking for something in them, weren't you?"

"Looking for something? Such as what?"

"Your Order of St. Isidore pendant, perhaps?"

Mr. Braithewaite's brow furrowed deeply. "My Order of St. Isidore pendant? No, I—"

"You gave it to Charlotte, am I correct?"

Mr. Braithewaite opened and closed his mouth and then let out a deep breath. "Well, yes, actually. It was a . . . a gift.

She saw it on my shelf one day and admired it, so I . . . I gave it to her. What of it?" He stood up and began pacing a little.

"You made her a gift of a pendant from a secret fraternal society? Does that not seem odd?"

"No, not . . . not really. What difference does it make? It's really none of your affair, Clive."

"You can stop playing the innocent, *Hugh*. We know all about your predilection for young waitresses at the club and your after-hours visits."

"This is outrageous! How dare you accuse me of such a thing, especially in the presence of a lady!" His eyes darted to Henrietta.

"Your consideration is admirable, Mr. Braithewaite, but I can assure you, I've heard much worse." Henrietta flashed him a knowing smile. "Let me guess what happened next. After Charlotte lost the pendant, she came home and told you about it and you panicked, drove to the club to retrieve the gifts to search through them."

"That's preposterous!" The veins in his neck bulged slightly. "Wait a moment. She lost it, you say? Surely not. She's a very . . . a very sensible sort of girl. She—"

"It was me," Beatrice said, quietly entering the study.

"Oh, Beatrice!" Henrietta exclaimed. "I thought you were out."

"No, I stayed behind."

"Beatrice, there is no need for you to be involved in this," Mr. Braithewaite said sternly. "You may leave us."

"But I *am* involved, Father." Her voice was quiet, and her face one of distinct sadness, or perhaps it was disappointment. "What he is saying is true," Beatrice said to Henrietta. "Well, partially true." There was an edge to Beatrice's voice that Henrietta had not heard before.

"When Charlotte told me that she had misplaced a necklace and then described it to me, I knew it was Father's. I also knew what it probably implied."

"Beatrice!"

"This sort of thing has happened before, has it not, Father? Maids, governesses, waitresses at the club—basically any young, impressionable woman. There have been older ones, too, but the young ones are Father's particular favorites," she said matter-of-factly to Henrietta and Clive, as if explaining a history lesson to them. "It has somehow fallen to me to cover up for him all these years, starting when I was just seventeen and discovered that our downstairs parlor maid had gotten herself 'in the family way' because of Father's nightly visits to the servants' wing. I was devastated, of course, by the shame of it, but I realized that poor Mother should never know. It would destroy her. Destroy all of us. So, I kept my discovery to myself—and all of the subsequent ones, as well." She walked to the window and absently looked out at the falling snow. "There have been several maids that have had to be let go over the years, haven't there, Father?" she asked without turning around. "Charlotte was simply the latest conquest. I knew that if the St. Isidore pendant was found in one of the boxes, Father might be found out. So, it was me who took Mother's keys and had myself driven back to the club that night. My intent was to go through the gifts while the driver waited, but then I realized it would be too big of a job, so I had our chauffeur help me load them all into the car."

"They all fit?"

"They didn't, unfortunately, so Noland brought the rest in a truck."

"I knew he was involved!" Clive muttered.

"You mustn't blame him. I swore him to secrecy. He helped me carry them all into the house. I stayed up the whole of the night unwrapping and rewrapping and then arranged for him to come the next day and take them back before the club opened. No one was the wiser. There are benefits, you see, to being a spinster daughter without the advantage of looks or suitors. No one takes much notice of what you do."

"Beatrice!" Mr. Braithewaite exclaimed.

"Did you find it?" Henrietta asked her.

Beatrice pulled the necklace from her skirt pocket and held it up briefly before setting it noiselessly on her father's desk. "There you are, Father."

Mr. Braithewaite stared at it. "Why! I . . ." he blustered. "You're all quite wrong, you know! There was nothing untoward between myself and Charlotte. It was an innocent gift on my part. Good God, she's the daughter of your mother's best friend."

"Which is all the more reason why it would have been so very painful. I will not see Mother hurt. Nor Charlotte. I'm quite fond of her myself. The sister I never had. And I couldn't stand by and let whatever reputation she does have be ruined by you."

Mr. Braithewaite, bristling, looked about to refute this but instead collapsed into the nearest chair, covering his face with one hand.

"I think it's time we should take our leave," Henrietta said quietly with a glance at Clive. "We'll see ourselves out." She gave Beatrice a faint smile.

Mr. Braithewaite did not comment and remained slumped in his chair with his face in his hands.

Beatrice led them to the front door. "I'm sorry to have caused you so much trouble," she said, her old meekness oddly returning. "You won't . . . you won't mention this to Mother, will you?"

Henrietta laid her hand on the girl's arm. "No, of course not."

"It's the reason I've never married, you see," she murmured. "Someone has to protect Mother."

Henrietta was of the opinion that Victoria Braithewaite was by no means in need of protecting, but then again, since Victoria's whole existence depended on social standing, Henrietta supposed Beatrice *was* protecting her in a way—from the shame and gossip her husband's dalliances might have caused over the years. This poor girl! Surrounded by every luxury and comfort and yet trapped by a web of deceit.

"Merry Christmas, Beatrice," Henrietta whispered in her ear as she embraced her. "You're always welcome to come stay with us in London, if you wish."

Beatrice pulled back, a sad smile tugging. "I don't know if Mother would let me go, and anyway, I'm needed here." She tilted her head back toward the study, where Hugh was probably still lamenting—or faux lamenting. It was hard to tell.

"Well, now that your father knows you know, he might think twice about . . . well, his actions, let's just say. Perhaps it's time for you to chart your own course." She brightened. "Why don't you come to London in the New Year for a long holiday?"

Henrietta could tell by the wistful look on the girl's face that she was intrigued by the suggestion.

"Mother will say I need a chaperone. Or worse, she'll want to come, too."

"Bring Charlotte as a companion, if you wish. Or I could ask my Aunt Agatha. She was my sister Elsie's companion for a time. She wasn't a very good one, though, so you needn't worry about her being too strict," Henrietta assured her with a little grin. "Elsie got away with all sorts."

Beatrice didn't say anything, but Henrietta could tell she was considering it.

"Well, you think about it. Write to me." She gave her another quick embrace and a kiss on the cheek. "Merry Christmas," she repeated. "And don't worry; your secret—or should I say your father's secret—is safe with us."

Henrietta took hold of Clive's arm, then, and the two of them stepped out into the snowy afternoon. The sky was a dull gray now, and the flakes had gotten smaller and faster, more determined in their descent. The Alfa was right where they had left it in the circled drive, though it was already covered in a light dusting of snow. Clive brushed it off with a gloved hand and after only a few false starts, got the car running. Henrietta twisted to look once more at the mansion as Clive pulled down the drive. Beatrice was still standing in the open doorway. She gave a little wave and then shut the door.

Henrietta turned back around.

"Don't say it," Clive said under his breath.

"But darling, you must give me some kind of credit. Can you not admit that I was right?"

"Yes, fine. You were right. But *I* was right about Peters," he said, shifting into a higher gear. "He *was* involved, *and* he was lying."

"Do you think Cummings knew?"

"Probably."

"You know, I feel sad for Charlotte as well in a certain way."

"Why? For being gullible?"

"Something like that, I guess." Henrietta looked out the window at all of the large estates they were passing, each bedecked with at the very least a fat Christmas wreath on the front door, and many had candles in the windows. "And then, of course, there's poor Beatrice," she said, turning back to Clive. "I can't imagine what her life has been like. To have Victoria as your mother, and Hugh as your father? No wonder she's so meek."

"But not as meek as she appears. It took some guts to stand up to Hugh today."

"True enough. I'll write to her when we get home and urge her to come."

"If you wish."

They passed a group of carolers who were walking from one house to the next. They were slipping and sliding in the new snow and were laughing as they made their way up the sidewalk of a charming Queen Anne. The sight of them made Henrietta long to see her own family. She wanted to laugh—really laugh—the way she only did with her brothers and sisters. Christmas Day at Highbury would be lavish and elegant and indulgent, but she simply couldn't wait for tomorrow to spend Christmas Eve with Elsie and Gunther and all the kids.

CHAPTER 13

Elsie looked at the clock hanging on the kitchen wall just above the sink for what seemed like the hundredth time. They would be here in a few hours, and she wasn't at all ready! Chef had scolded her twice for getting in the way, but Elsie wasn't sure how everything was going to be finished in time.

The vegetables, for example, were still lying raw on the center chopping table, and Nellie, Chef's assistant, seemed to be taking her leisure as she rolled out pastry. Old Odelia had been pressed into service to wash pots, a task she seemed quite resentful of, and Karl, as usual, was not much help, shuffling from task to task as if it were any ordinary day and not Christmas Eve!

Elsie looked down at the tomato aspic in front of her. It was the one thing she had offered to prepare for the big dinner tonight, as it was normally her specialty, but this one had, of course, somehow failed to come out. Perhaps it was worry on her part, or the constant interruptions she had had whilst making it, or more than likely, the heat of the kitchen, which was causing it to be a bit weepy. She tried dotting the plate with holly leaves, thinking it would make it look more Christmasy, but the aspic itself was a peculiar shade of deep orange rather than a cherry red, and not even the addition of holly leaves could transform it into something appropriate for the Christmas table, as it looked like something more suitable for Thanksgiving. She sighed and carried it to the icebox. Maybe it just needed more firming up.

"Elsie!" Donny came bursting into the room, looking eagerly, Elsie could tell, around for any cakes with frosting he might sample with a swipe of a pudgy finger. "Ma wants you!"

Elsie groaned. Not again. Ma seemed more than unusually cantankerous today, which was typical. Holidays always seemed to bring on her nerves. Elsie handed the aspic platter to Nellie and ignored the girl's scowl when she told her to "find a place in the icebox for this, would you, Nellie?" knowing as she did that the icebox was already overstuffed.

Elsie followed Donny down the short hallway and through to the dining room, where Karl was lazily setting the table—still! She considered suggesting to him that he perhaps hurry up, but she refrained, knowing that it wouldn't do any good, and instead followed Donny up the stairs and down the long hallway to Ma's bedroom at the very end. Not exactly the "mad woman in the attic," but not too far off, Elsie had often mused, in more ways than one. She gave a quick knock and found Ma sitting, as usual, by the window in her ratty old armchair—the one thing she had insisted on bringing from their shabby apartment on Armitage.

"Yes, Ma?" Elsie gave the nurse, Miss Flanagan, a quick glance. She responded with rolled eyes and a quick shake of her head.

"Who's coming today, Elsie?" Ma snapped. "This one says it's Henrietta." She jabbed a thumb over her shoulder at the nurse.

"It *is* Henrietta, Ma. Remember?"

Ma's eyes grew wide. "You never told me that!"

Elsie let out an exasperated breath. She really didn't have time for one of Ma's "spells." Not today, with the guests arriving so soon! "I did, Ma."

"No, you didn't!" Ma cried, her voice growing louder.

Miss Flanagan stepped from behind the chair. "Well, whether you knew or not, won't it be nice to see her, Mrs. Von Harmon?" she said soothingly.

Ma's forehead crinkled in confusion. "I s'pose. But I thought she was in Europe."

Elsie was actually somewhat impressed that Ma remembered this much. "She was, Ma. But she's home for a visit. For Christmas."

"Christmas? It isn't Christmas! Is it?" She gave the window a worried glance, as if the answer lay outside.

"It's Christmas Eve, Ma. Yes, it is," she said in response to Ma's shaking of her head.

"I think you're wrong there, Elsie," Ma grumbled, "but you won't listen to me."

"Come, come, Mrs. Von Harmon," Miss Flanagan intervened. "Let's put on something special, should we? We'll let Elsie be on her way. She has a lot to do today, I'm sure."

"Elsie? Elsie doesn't do anything!" Ma said bitterly as Miss Flanagan wrapped her arm under hers to help her to stand.

Elsie let out a little sigh and turned to go. Though she was used to Ma's bitter barbs—*hadn't she been hearing them for most of her life?*—they were still effective at stinging her no matter how much she tried to ignore them. She gave Miss Flanagan a grateful look and stepped back into the hallway, where Donny was leaning with his backside against the wall. It pained her that neither Doris nor Donny wanted to spend much time in their mother's presence, as if they were afraid of her. Elsie straightened his tie. "What is it?" she asked, knowing that he must want something, or he would have scampered off by now.

"Jimmy won't play with me," he whined. "He says I'm a baby."

Elsie sighed again. The boys had arrived home from boarding school last night, filling the house with boisterous laughter and shouts, which had made her achingly realize how much she missed them. Eddie had filled out nicely and, at age sixteen, was nearly grown. He was tall and broad and had apparently joined the rugby team as well as the polo team at Phillips Exeter. He had retained his mischievous spirit, though, and laughed easily. Herbie, in contrast, was rail-thin—the spitting image of their father. He was just as quiet as ever and had somehow acquired glasses, as well as a slight cough, and had sat up very late with Gunther last night discussing politics and philosophy, which, of course, had pleased Gunther immensely. And then there was Jimmy, who at age eight, was closer to Donny and Doris's age than Herbie's, but who seemed to want little to do with his younger siblings, which partially broke Elsie's heart. Jimmy, always the sweetest of the bunch, seemed to have lost much of his charming innocence in the short time that he had been gone.

"Well, why don't you show him your new train? He's always loved trains."

"I did, but he said he doesn't care 'bout that no more. That toys are for babies." Donny's lower lip wobbled.

"Oh, I think he's just putting on airs." She gave him a little smile. "He'll come round. You'll see." Elsie ruffled his hair. "Why don't you show him the cats?"

"I already did." Donny pouted and crossed his arms.

Elsie rolled her eyes and began to stride down the hallway, gently pulling Donny along with her. She didn't have time for this. "We'll worry about Jimmy later. Where are Doris and Anna?"

"With the cats."

"Go down and find them and tell them its time to get dressed. It's almost time for Henrietta and Clive and baby Teddy to arrive!"

"Aw, gee. How come I gotta do everything?" He pouted again.

"Well, I'd do as I was told if I were you," Elsie warned. "Santa comes tonight, don't forget."

Donny's eyes widened, and he promptly ran down the back staircase, which led directly into the kitchen. The cats—Tom and Irene, that is—were now safely housed in a nest of straw and blankets on the back porch off the kitchen, which was warm and pleasant, and which, in keeping them out of the house proper, had thus far prevented an allergic reaction in Gunther. It was he, in fact, who had insisted—once Elsie had had a chance to explain amidst the cries of joy from the children when she and Mr. Ferguson and Tom and *another* cat had shuffled in from the cold not three nights ago—that Mr. Ferguson stay with them until arrangements of some sort could be made.

And while the cats had been rather conveniently lodged on the back porch, Mr. Ferguson, conversely, was a bit more of a problem, as he had found it nearly impossible to climb the stairs to any of the guest rooms proper. Instead, Gunther, who, like Elsie, seemed to have a particular empathy for strays—having been a sort of one himself not so very long ago—had cleverly devised a way to convert the back parlor into a temporary bedroom of sorts. Mr. Ferguson, for his part, seemed not to mind the inconvenience, if it could be called that, at all. Indeed, he was proving not to be a very demanding houseguest in any sense of the word, nor, however, was he a very interesting one. He needed little, it seemed, in the way of entertainment and was content to sit beside the fireplace, a blanket tucked around his knees, for the better part of a day. He would be, Elsie ruminated, perhaps a good companion for Ma if Ma would ever leave her room. As it was, getting her down the stairs today was going to be a stretch . . .

Elsie hurried down the main staircase and into the front drawing room now to make sure everything was just so. They had planned to purchase a little Douglas fir from the lot up on Fullerton, but before they had had a chance, Grandfather had arrived, like a repentant Scrooge, with a magnificent balsam fir that practically filled the whole room. He had had his men carry it in and set it up, of course, and had then departed, despite Elsie's earnest pleas for him to remain for dinner. He was a frequent guest for dinner now, and accordingly, Elsie had begged him to come to Christmas Eve, wanting Henrietta to see for herself his astounding transformation, to which he had happily agreed. Just this morning, however, he had telephoned to say that he had succumbed to a cold and that his doctor had advised him to remain in bed and that he thus would not be attending after all. Elsie was sorely disappointed, of course, but she promised him that she and Gunther and the children would pay him a visit on Christmas Day instead.

Elsie straightened a couple of the ornaments on the tree, and checked, one more time, to see if there were enough candles. They had never had a tree this big, and, truth be told, it was a little bare. But, Elsie mused, they would accumulate more ornaments as the years went along. They would light the candles tonight and maybe sing carols round it. *Would Clive like to sing carols?* Oh! What did it matter? It was Christmas after all! The one time of the year that sentimentality could be forgiven.

Gunther strode in, his hands in his pockets, a grin creeping up his face as his eyes alighted on Elsie. He gently took her hands in his and kissed her on the forehead, an act which still caused her heart to thrill a bit, as they were, in truth—though so much had happened and though they already had such a full household—still newlyweds.

"Merry Christmas, *Liebling*. You are lovelier than a Christmas angel. In fact, you *are* an angel."

"Gunther!" she exclaimed, trying to hide her smile. "That's sacrilegious."

He laughed. "That I do not know. But what I do know is that it is true. I love you, Elsie." He kissed her lips. "This is the happiest Christmas I have ever known, and that is because of you."

"Oh, Gunther!" She was surprised by his rare expression of emotion and, wanting to savor it, gently laid her head against his chest and let herself briefly rest. "I'm so worried about tonight," she mumbled after a few moments of respite. "I want everything to be perfect."

"It will be. It already is."

"But what if the turkey isn't cooked through?" She pulled away, and his hands went around her waist. She rubbed her forehead. "I really don't think it will be done in time."

"I have not yet known Chef to fail."

When Elsie did not respond, Gunther smiled and rubbed a finger against her cheek. "Christmas, I believe, is not about turkey and trees, is that not so?"

For a second or two, she was tempted to give in to this reasoning, but she resisted. "But what about Mr. Ferguson? As we've seen, he . . . he doesn't exactly have what I'd call proper table manners. And what about the Hennesseys? They—"

Gunther put a finger to her lips and gazed at her with that steadying look of his. She felt herself melt a little in the warmth of his deep blue eyes. "The Christ child was born in a stable, Elsie. With animals and dirty straw and manure. And we are not better than Him. We would be wise to remember this through all the year, not just at Christmas."

Elsie gave him a little frown. She knew he was right, of course, but still . . .

"Henrietta is your sister," he went on. "She will not judge ill of you if the potatoes are undercooked, or the presents not perfect, or the spirit found wanting. Nor will Clive," he added, somehow guessing the real cause of her despair. "He's already been here, so I have been told, for Christmas, and it was not then a cause for such tribulation. Clive is a sensible man. He is not swayed by wealth and influence. This is why he chose to be a city detective, no? He has seen much worse things than what he will find here today, *Liebling*. Is this not so?"

"Oh, Gunther, I suppose you're right. I'm just being silly! I just want everything to be—"

"They're here!" Donny shouted, running past the drawing room in a race with Jimmy, who easily pulled the lead, Doris following. Anna, in turn, ran to Gunther, her arms outstretched, and he dutifully picked her up. She immediately put a finger in her mouth as she looked warily at the front door. Elsie understood the girl's reaction, but at five years old, she was too old to be held like a baby, despite her tiny size, but now was not the time to correct it. Gently, though, she tapped Anna's hand from her mouth and strode to the door and threw it open.

There, standing on the cement porch, after all these long months, was Henrietta! She was dressed in a modest navy-blue woolen coat and matching hat, and in her arms was a perfect cherub of a baby, his cheeks pink and his tiny blond curls sticking out from the hat securely strapped under his chin, his eyes wide as he stared at the small group at the door. Clive, weighed down with several gifts in his arms, beamed from behind them.

"Merry Christmas!" Henrietta said gaily. "Oh, Merry Christmas! It's so good to see all of you!"

"Oh, Henrietta! Come in, come in!" Elsie stepped aside and gestured for them to enter.

The Howards gingerly stepped inside and in so doing set off an immediate cascade of embraces, kisses, and shouts of welcome as more and more of the siblings ran from all parts of the house to greet their big sister. Fritz, weighed down with another pile of gifts, slipped in behind them and followed Karl, who had finally appeared from somewhere deeper in the house, to the drawing room to deposit them under the tree.

"Oh, Hen, he's so beautiful!" Elsie exclaimed as Henrietta unsnapped the strap of his navy-blue cap and pulled it off, his little blond curls sticking up with static.

Henrietta laughed her pretty laugh as she smoothed Teddy's hair. "We rather think so," she said, tossing a look back at Clive, who grinned at her. Bewildered, Teddy stared at what was probably the largest group of people he had ever encountered in one room. He thrust his little fist in his mouth and burrowed his face into Henrietta's neck.

"He's shy. He'll come round in a couple of minutes." She smiled at everyone. "My! Look at all of you!"

"Eddie, take those gifts into the drawing room," Elsie instructed, nodding to the stack still in Clive's arms.

"Thank you, Ed," Clive said, handing them to the young man and then removing his coat. Karl was still in the other room with Fritz, so he draped it over one arm and held his other out to Gunther. "Merry Christmas."

"And to you, Lord Linley." Gunther managed to shake Clive's hand despite still having Anna in his arms.

"Don't be soft, man. Clive."

"Clive, then. Here, Anna, get down now." Gunther placed the girl gently on the ground, and she immediately hid behind his leg, an action which seemed to catch Teddy's attention. He raised his head.

"Oh, Henrietta! Doesn't he look just like Grandfather?" Elsie gushed. "I think he definitely takes after the Exley side, don't you? Or maybe it's the Von Harmons?"

Henrietta laughed. "Antonia thinks he looks like the Howards. Oh, who knows? I suppose he looks like himself. Are we the first to arrive?" Henrietta said, looking around. "Oh, Elsie! You've made this place a real home! Everything is lovely."

Elsie felt a rush of pride. "Oh! Well. Thank you. I try. I've added a few things here and there . . ." She gripped her hands tightly.

"And look at all of you!" Henrietta repeated, admiring her brothers, who were all dressed smartly in woolen slacks, argyle vests, ties, and blazers, except Jimmy and Donny, of course, who were still in short pants and long socks. Henrietta kissed Eddie and Herbie each on the cheek. "You two are practically men now! And Jimmy! You've grown, too. How on earth did you get so tall?" She ruffled his hair, and he grinned at her, the old Jimmy peeking through.

"Oh, Hen!" he cried, wrapping his arms around her mid-section. "I missed you!"

She bent down and kissed him on the head and then opened her free arm to Doris and Donny, who were hovering near Elsie. "Come here, you two! Don't you have a hug for your big sister? I've brought you something from London!"

Donny looked excitedly at Doris, and the two dashed forward and gripped her around the middle.

"And something for Anna, too," Henrietta called to the shadow still hiding behind Gunther's leg. "And Jimmy, and all of you." She threw a smile toward Eddie and Herbie. "And where's Ma?" Henrietta asked, looking around the room. "Upstairs, still?"

"Yes, she'll be down later. We'll have to help her. She can't really climb the stairs anymore."

"Everyone, let us proceed to front parlor." Gunther gestured toward the adjacent room. "We will have sherry before dinner."

"Come look at our tree, Hen," Donny urged, taking Henrietta's free hand and pulling her. "It's the biggest one you ever seen!"

"I'll just be a moment," Elsie said to no one in particular and hurried off toward the kitchen to check Chef's progress and feeling for the first time that the evening just might turn out okay.

Henrietta allowed herself to be led to the tree, utterly pleased with how the evening was thus far unfolding. It was wonderful to be home, though this had never really been *her* home, having grown up in the shabby apartment on Armitage and remaining there almost all the way up until the moment she had married Clive. Nonetheless, it was wonderful to be among them all, and she didn't think anything could mar her happiness tonight.

She made much of all the ornaments for the benefit of Donny and Doris and even Anna, who had also crept close. She was touched by the fact that Elsie had interspersed some of their old homemade ones with all of the new, shiny glass ones that adorned the tree. Even Teddy seemed interested and reached out a hand to try to grab a shiny red drum.

"He must want a drum for Christmas, don't he, Hen?" Donny asked eagerly, reaching up and rubbing Teddy's back. He seemed particularly intrigued with his baby nephew.

Henrietta was about to answer but was interrupted by a very loud knocking at the door.

"That would be the Hennesseys." Gunther set down the bottle of sherry he was holding. "I will go." Somehow, however, Karl must have been in the vicinity of the front door because before Gunther even made it across the room, Mrs. Hennessey barged into the parlor accompanied by a grinning Mr. Hennessey.

"Oh, my! Traffic's terrible with the snow!" Mrs. Hennessey exclaimed as she hurriedly peeled off her things and handed them to Karl, who had sleepily trailed in behind them like a stray dog himself. "And where's Henrietta? And where's that baby? Ah!" Mrs. Hennessey cried, spotting Henrietta by the tree and making a beeline for her. "There he is! Let me have a little hold of him!" She promptly snatched Teddy from her arms. "Oh! Look at him! Ain't he you all over, Henrietta!"

Teddy immediately began to cry, but rather than hand him back, Mrs. Hennessey whisked him off and tried to quiet him by showing him different objects around the room. Eventually, his wails turned into little hiccups, but he still looked forlornly at Henrietta and whined. Henrietta wasn't sure what to do.

"Hello, girl," Mr. Hennessey said gently, and in the moment, Henrietta was distracted from her concern for Teddy by a burst of love. She had forgotten how much she missed her old boss—dare she say father? She wrapped her arms around him.

"Hello, Mr. Hennessey," she mumbled into his thick tweed jacket, which carried the scent of years of tobacco smoke and stale beer. "You're looking well."

"As are you, girl. As are you."

Mrs. Hennessey returned with her captive, who practically lurched himself into Henrietta's arms and then buried his face in her neck once she had hold of him again. She began to sway slightly to soothe him.

"Motherhood fits her, don't it, William? You're a natural, girl. I can tell. Always thought you'd be good. Well, how could you not be? Had so much practice with this lot," she said, looking pleasantly around the room. "Now, which one are you?" she asked Donny.

Clive approached, holding out his hand. "Mr. Hennessey," he said, shaking it firmly. "Merry Christmas. Lovely to see you."

"Mrs. Hennessey," he said with a deferential nod. "Merry Christmas."

"You ain't gettin' away with that!" Mrs. Hennessey declared. "Come give me a hug!"

Henrietta bit back a smile, noticing Clive's cheeks flush slightly as he obeyed the older woman, who now grasped him tightly around the neck.

"That's better! Elsie's been writin' to us. Tells us you're a duke or a count or something like that now! I never!"

One of Clive's eyes squinted shut, and Henrietta could tell he was trying to keep his composure.

"A lord, to be exact," he answered, a small smile escaping despite his best efforts. "But it's really just a title. It doesn't mean anything."

"Oh! A lord! That's fancy an' all, ain't it, William? We'll have to watch our p's and q's around this one now!" She cackled with laughter. "Might end up as the king someday! Wouldn't that be a cracker? An American as the King of England? Good lord—oooh!" she laughed, "I made a joke without even intendin' to!"

"Oh, hello, Mr. and Mrs. Hennessey," Elsie said happily, reentering the room now. "You're just in time. Dinner is ready!"

Though the Palmer Square dining room was quite large, it was a bit of a tight squeeze to fit not only Clive and Henrietta, but Mr. and Mrs. Hennessey and Mr. Ferguson as well, who was already oddly seated at the table when the rest of the guests entered and whom Gunther politely introduced as their "neighbor." Henrietta thought the addition odd, as Elsie had not mentioned that she was inviting a neighbor, but noting his threadbare suit coat and slightly unshaven face, she assumed it was yet another of Elsie's strays.

Ma, too, took up a bit of extra room with her wheelchair. Eddie and Herbie carried it down for her and dutifully wheeled her in. Henrietta, her stomach clenching with nervousness as to how Ma would react to her and Clive and Teddy, her first true grandchild, was instead aghast by the sight of what was essentially a gaunt, shrunken woman. If she didn't know better, Henrietta would have guessed her to be decades older than she really was. Gone was the stout, formidable woman in her memory. She was shocked by how much her mother had aged. She would have thought that living in luxury now in Palmer Square would have made her happy and robust, stronger than ever, but in truth it seemed to have done the opposite. All the fight had gone out of her. Henrietta quickly recalled Elsie mentioning this in letters, but she hadn't realized the extent of Ma's decline.

"Merry Christmas, Ma!" Henrietta gushed as she hurried over with Teddy. "Would you like to meet your grandson? This is Teddy," she said, smoothing his hair.

Ma's cloudy eyes looked him over, but she did not react. "You coming back home now, Henrietta? Elsie could use the help. Not fair on her."

"Well, we're home for a little while, Ma. I'm hoping to visit a lot while I'm here." Henrietta shifted Teddy onto her hip, regretting the time she had already wasted at the club with the missing gifts. That seemed a whole other world, and a silly one at that.

"Elsie, fix my chair!" Ma snapped. "This ain't right." Ma's bony, veiny fingers bounced along the table edge. "I'm not close enough."

"Here, I'll try, Ma," Eddie said, trying to push the chair closer.

"No, that ain't right, either."

"Allow me," Gunther said calmly, coming around to where Eddie was still trying to adjust Ma's chair, his face flushed with the effort. "How she likes it, I know."

Gunther shifted the chair imperceptibly to the right, which seemed to oddly satisfy Ma, who reached then for her napkin and haphazardly laid it on her lap. She sat slumped, staring absently at the empty chair across from her. She seemed to have forgotten that Henrietta was standing there, so Henrietta saw nothing more to do but awkwardly move away and search the table for her place card, her face burning slightly. She was tempted to give in to the hurt she felt, but she pushed it away, determined to be happy on Christmas Eve, and tried to put it down to Ma's advanced aging. She resolved to discuss it with Elsie, though, who sadly, she realized fully now, had to deal with Ma every day.

She finally spotted *Henrietta* written out in Elsie's neat, calligraphic script at a corner seat on Gunther's left. Slightly behind her chair, angled between her and Gunther, she noticed a strange contraption that resembled a type of baby highchair. It looked positively ancient—probably Victorian—a relic they must have unearthed in the attic and carried down. Henrietta was touched by their thoughtfulness, but she wasn't at all sure that the chair would not collapse under the weight of an actual human baby and not, say, a doll. She would rather just hold Teddy on her lap, but she didn't want to offend her hosts, so she gingerly eased Teddy into the contraption, fully expecting to have to snatch him back when it broke under him. Miraculously, though, it seemed to hold his weight, at least for now. Warily, she lowered herself onto her own chair and glanced down the table at Clive for reassurance, but he was already in a conversation with Herbie to his right.

Gunther finally took his place at the head of the table, and Elsie, giving him what looked like a grateful smile, took her seat opposite him at the other end. Henrietta, surreptitiously observing the two of them, could not think of a better-matched couple. Elsie, though still soft-spoken and quiet, seemed to have grown into her role as not only a wife and a mother figure, but also the head of the household—so much that Henrietta could hardly believe it. Gone was her insecure, shy little sister and in her place had appeared a confident, lovely young woman. And Gunther, for his part, looked every bit the professor. He had grown a little stouter since they had last seen him and his beard was fuller, but it suited him.

Elsie signaled Karl now, who in turn poked his head around the swinging door to inform the staff inevitably huddled on the other side that dinner had begun. He and Nellie then began carrying in the first course, which was celery filled with pimento cheese and ripe olives, followed by a shallow bowl of cream of almond soup.

"Never had nut soup before, have we, William?" Mrs. Hennessey declared after sampling several bites. "Not bad." She took another slurp. "But not what I'd-a thought for Christmas. Maybe something like good ole chicken noodle."

"Chef suggested it. It's French, I think." Elsie shot a nervous glance at Clive, but her look was lost on him, as he was now discussing polo with Eddie.

"Well, I think it's delicious," Henrietta said. "We had it in Paris, and this is every bit as good."

The first courses were followed by slices of turkey and gravy, mashed potatoes, apple-and-raisin stuffing, baked spiced oranges, cranberry-nut sauce, buttered peas and carrots, tiny powdered biscuits, a droopy tomato aspic, and a persimmon salad. Henrietta, in truth, was impressed with the menu and was proud of Elsie.

Gunther, as kind and thoughtful as ever, seemed particularly adept at keeping the conversation going, being able to discuss almost any subject at length as well as having a knack for drawing people into the discussion, though this particular skill was in no way needed with Mrs. Hennessey, who needed little, if any, encouragement to speak. In fact, she quite dominated the conversation several times and regaled them with stories of their daughter, Winifred, whose own child, Prudence Fern, all of three years old, was already reading and could do basic arithmetic. She was, apparently, quite a child prodigy.

"They're awfully strict with her, though, ain't they, William?" the good woman said, relating the one and only time they had been allowed to go visit the budding family out East. "I tried to tell her, but a-course she don't listen to me. Still. We're awfully proud of our Winifred, ain't we, William?"

"Do you see much of Stan?" Henrietta asked, trying to discreetly feed some mashed potatoes to Teddy. She was not used to feeding him in such a formal, public setting, and she wasn't sure how she was to proceed, given that she, or Edna, truth be told, usually fed him in the kitchen whilst wearing an apron, not a dark-green Chanel. She knew, though, from experience that tomorrow Antonia would not hear of having any children at her dinner table, Christmas or no. Teddy would *have* to have his Christmas dinner upstairs in the nursery with Randy and Howard, so she was determined to enjoy his presence here tonight, even though it meant spilled potatoes on her gown.

"Stan?" Mrs. Hennessey paused to take a bite of her roast turkey, taking care to first dip it in the rich gravy pooling around her plate. "See him all the time," she mumbled between the food in her mouth. "Well, actually, it's Rose we see the most. She works at Poor Pete's weekend nights, don't she, William? Got *yer* old job, girl!" She laughed.

"Stan was promoted to foreman at the Electrics," Mr. Hennessey put in. "Good lad, he is."

"Did they find a place?" Henrietta asked, wiping Teddy's mouth.

"Not yet. Still with his parents. Said they could live with us, didn't we, William? But they said, no, like. Why don't you give 'im some carrots, Henrietta? Mash some up there on yer plate."

Henrietta bit the inside of her cheek. "No, he's fine, Mrs. Hennessey," she replied over her shoulder.

"It's dead easy. Here. Want me to do it for you? Give me some of your carrots, William. I ate all mine."

"No, really, Mrs. Hennessey. He's fine. He hasn't had carrots yet, and I don't want to try it now." In truth, she wasn't sure whether Edna had given him carrots or not.

"Not had carrots? Why not?" Mrs. Hennessey asked incredulously. "They're the best thing goin' for babies. Here," she began mashing the carrots she had slid off the plate Mr. Hennessey had handed her. "Nothin' to it."

"Thanks, Mrs. Hennessey, but I don't want to give him something new on Christmas Eve in case it upsets his stomach."

"Upset his stomach? They won't—"

"Tell me, Doris," Clive interrupted. "What do you hope Santa will bring?" Henrietta threw him a grateful look, to which he responded with a slight wink.

"A dolly and a buggy!" Doris chirped.

"Ah!" Clive said, shooting her a smile. "And what about you, Donny?"

"I want a new caboose for my train set!"

"Good choice. What about you, Anna?" Clive asked kindly.

Anna bit her lips together and shot a frightened look at Elsie, who responded with an encouraging nod. "Tell him what you want, Anna." Her tone was warm and calm.

Everyone waited patiently for the girl to answer.

"A kitty," she murmured and then promptly leaned over and put her head under the table. Elsie gently pulled her upright, putting her arm around her.

"I want a BB gun," announced Jimmy.

"A BB gun!" Elsie exclaimed.

"All the boys have 'em at school, don't they, Ed?"

"Well, some do," his older brother agreed. "I wouldn't take one, though. It'll just get pinched."

"But you're not goin' back, are you?" Donny asked, looking at each of his brothers in turn. "Grandfather says you don't have to now."

All three of the older boys shifted uncomfortably. "Well, I—" Herbie began.

"We'll discuss it later, why don't we?" Elsie put in. "It's Christmas Eve! No serious subjects! Let's have dessert," she said, signaling Karl, "and then we'll go into the parlor."

"Can we play charades again this year?" Jimmy begged. "And sing carols?"

"Well . . . if everyone wants to." Elsie looked around the table cautiously, and Henrietta noticed she avoided looking directly at Clive.

"Of course we do!" Henrietta said enthusiastically, answering for both of them.

"That'll do us, won't it, William? Though it's been years since we played anything like that." Mrs. Hennessey leaned back in her chair. "What you got for dessert, Elsie?"

"I thought we'd have a traditional plum pudding," she said, this time glancing nervously at Clive. "Chef assures me that he knows how to make it. I so apologize if it's wrong."

"Plum pudding?" Mrs. Hennessey said incredulously. "We always have apple pie, don't we, William? Don't know if it'll seem like Christmas without apple pie."

Elsie's face fell. "Well, I just thought . . ."

"I'm sure it will be delicious," Gunther said soothingly. "Don't you agree, Mr. Ferguson?"

At the sound of his name, Mr. Ferguson put down the plate he was currently licking and vigorously nodded. "Oh, aye. That'll do me." It was the first words he had spoken all evening.

Henrietta bit back a smile as she extracted Teddy from the chair and placed him on her lap just as Nellie entered with thick slices of plum pudding covered with rich brandy sauce and began setting them in front of each person. Karl entered with a coffee cart. Teddy began to squirm and fuss. He would need nursing soon, Henrietta worried, and took a quick bite of the plum pudding while she could.

"Perfect, Elsie," Clive complimented. "Just like in England. Do you have the same cook as last year? He's outdone himself." Henrietta was grateful that he had apparently noticed Elsie's unease. He surprised her sometimes with his attention to small details, but, then again, he *was* a detective . . .

Teddy began to actually cry now. Henrietta stood up with him. "Please excuse me," she apologized.

"Nursin' him, eh? Well, I wondered," Mrs. Hennessey said, taking a large mouthful of the plum pudding. "Best thing for 'im, ain't it, William? Winifred's still nursing Prudence, an' she's three!"

"Here, let me help you," Elsie said, rising as well.

Henrietta was about to protest the need for assistance, but then realized this might be her only chance to speak privately with her sister. "Yes, that would be nice, Elsie. Thank you."

Elsie led her down the hallway toward the back parlor, but then stopped. "Oh, I forgot. Mr. Ferguson's things are in there." She led her instead to the library. It was a quarter of the size of Highbury's library, but it was cozy just the same. "Here, hold him a moment, would you?" Henrietta asked, trying to undo her gown. "Chanel gowns aren't conducive to nursing," she said with a little laugh.

Elsie took the crying Teddy and tried to soothe him by rocking him. "He reminds me a little of Jimmy when he was a baby," she said over his cries. "Remember how colicky he was? Ma wouldn't get up with him, so we had to."

Henrietta reached for Teddy and nestled him against her chest.

"You're a wonderful mother, Hen. But then I always knew you would be."

Henrietta continued to adjust Teddy. "Thanks, Els. I don't always feel like it." Teddy finally latched on, and Henrietta's shoulders relaxed a little. "And I have help. Who knows if I would be able to do it without Edna."

"Course you would! You took care of all of us."

"No, *you* did."

Elsie laughed. "Okay, we both did."

"Speaking of mothering, any little announcement you'd like to make?"

Elsie's face flushed. "No, not yet."

"Don't worry. It will come."

"I hope so, though sometimes I think it might be God's way of saving my sanity. I already have enough to handle, especially with classes."

"I don't know how you find the time."

"Well, I have help, too." She smiled. "Just think, if all goes to plan, I'll be a teacher in just two years!"

"Do you miss living on campus? Being on your own?"

"Not at all." Elsie laughed. "Though I do miss Melody. But she's not there anymore anyway." Melody Merriweather was her flirtatious roommate and self-proclaimed very best friend.

"Yes, I seem to remember you wrote something about her in one of your letters."

"Her father had a heart attack, so she had to go back home to Wisconsin and help."

Henrietta adjusted Teddy. "Well, maybe she'll return at some point."

"I'm not sure. She seems entrenched there at the moment. Her letters are fantastically funny. She seems to get herself into the oddest scrapes."

"Speaking of entrenched, what are you going to do with this Mr. Ferguson? Where'd you dig him up?"

Elsie sighed. "He showed up one night looking for his missing cat. I walked him home, and, oh, Hen, it was pitiful. No heat, no electricity. I couldn't just leave him there!"

"Well, what are you going to do with him?" Henrietta raised her eyebrows.

Elsie sighed again. "Gunther is looking into finding a place. We may have to involve Grandfather. The poor old thing is no trouble, though, and the children love the cats he came with, especially Anna."

"She seems better. Brighter, I think."

"Yes, being around Doris and Donny is really helping her, I think."

"What about her fits?"

"She hasn't had one in a long time. The cold seems to ward them off."

"And what about Ma?"

Elsie let out a little sigh. "What about her?"

"She seems terrible."

"She *is* terrible. She's aged terrifically, Henrietta. And her mind grows dimmer every day. Thank God for Miss Flanagan; otherwise, I might lose my mind. I did try to tell you in letters."

"I know you did," she said, reaching out a hand. "I'm sorry. I guess I just didn't realize how bad she'd gotten."

Teddy pulled away and sleepily looked over at Elsie.

"I miss you, Hen."

"I miss you, too, Elsie." She squeezed her hand and then let it drop. "Someday I want you to come and stay with us."

"I'd like that. Not just yet, though. But someday."

The two sisters sat in companionable silence for a few moments before Elsie reluctantly stood. "Well, I suppose I should get back. Do you think Clive really wants to play charades?"

"Of course he does," Henrietta insisted, hoping that a white lie on Christmas Eve would be forgiven. "He's not so stuffy as you imagine. You never used to be worried about him, did you?"

"No, I suppose not. But somehow him becoming Lord Linley and me practically being in charge of the house, I just felt . . . well, I just wanted everything to be perfect."

"It *is* perfect, Elsie. Truly. Everything is lovely." Again, she marveled at how much Elsie had changed. "Are you happy with Gunther?" she asked softly. "You seem to be."

A faint blush crept over Elsie's face as she stood in the doorway, gripping the side of the door. "Yes. Very." She smiled shyly.

"You'd tell me if you . . . if you weren't, wouldn't you?" Henrietta sat Teddy up and rubbed his back, hoping he would burp.

"Of course I would, Hen. But there is no need. I'm happier than I have ever been." Elsie gave her sister another quick smile and then hurried out.

Left alone in the darkened room, Henrietta felt a burst of joy that Elsie had finally found happiness after all that she had been through. Under her and Gunther's rule, the house seemed to be such a happy, open one, filled with much laughter and discussion, and for just a fleeting moment, Henrietta felt a tiny whisp of envy that their own house in London was so much more staid and quiet—proper and elegant. *This* was the type of household she wished she and Clive could have, but she dispelled these thoughts quickly and tried to be grateful for all that they *did* have.

The rest of the evening seemed to fly by. The inevitable game of charades was played, as were several rounds of twenty questions, followed by a little Christmas sing-along with the aid of the Victrola and all of the Christmas records that Jimmy and Ed had hauled out from the cabinet beneath it. Presents were finally exchanged, to the great delight of all, and then, near midnight, Clive and Henrietta begged their leave, as Teddy was already sound asleep.

"Oh! Please stay, Hen!" Donny begged. "Teddy can sleep in my room," he offered as Henrietta bent to give him a hug.

"No, we have to go," Henrietta said wistfully, tousling his hair.

"But why?" he whined.

"'Cause if we don't, Santa will be confused, won't he? He won't know where to leave our gifts—here or there. And he might get yours mixed up then, too." Henrietta was aware that this logic didn't really make sense, but it was late, and Donny was little—and overtired. "In fact," she continued seriously. "If we don't all get to sleep, he won't come at all! That happened to us one year, didn't it, Elsie?" She threw a glance to her sister, who knew as well as Henrietta did that that was not the reason why Santa had not come to them during several lean years.

"Yes, indeed!" Elsie agreed. "Now hurry up! Say good-bye and get upstairs."

"Good-bye!" the four youngest (Jimmy having finally joined leagues with them) shouted, fresh enthusiasm coursing through them. "Good-bye, Hen! Good-bye, Clive! Good-bye, Teddy!" They raced each other for the stairs, while Henrietta hugged and kissed the older ones. The last person Henrietta said good-bye to was Ma, who had miraculously remained awake for the whole of the evening . . . well, mostly awake.

"Good-bye, Ma," Henrietta said, leaning down to awkwardly embrace her mother.

"You comin' tomorrow?" Ma asked.

Henrietta's stomach clenched. "Not tomorrow, Ma. We're spending it with Clive's family."

Ma stared straight ahead, as she seemed to have a habit of doing, and nodded absently, as if trying to take this in. "Got a real good baby, there, Henrietta. What's his name again?"

"Teddy."

"Teddy. Teddy. Well, he's a real good baby. Doesn't cry much. He looks like my father."

Henrietta was shocked by this observation, as she didn't think Ma had even really been aware of him. "Well, that's what Elsie said."

"It's a shame Grandfather couldn't be here tonight," Elsie put in, laying a hand on Henrietta's arm. "He told me to wish you and Clive a very merry Christmas."

"Thank you, Elsie," Henrietta said, wrapping her arms around her sister. "Please tell him the same. We've had such a perfect time with all of you. Thank you for the lovely Christmas party." She hugged her tightly.

"Merry Christmas," Elsie whispered into her ear. Henrietta felt in danger of crying, though she wasn't sure why.

"Darling, we should go," Clive said gently, stepping back into the house. He had ducked out with all of the gifts they had been given and had likewise pulled the Alfa up from where he had parked it down the street. "The car's running . . ."

"Yes, of course." She gingerly picked up Teddy, asleep on the sofa. Elsie draped his blanket over him.

"Good-bye, everyone! Merry Christmas!" she called softly, careful not to wake the sleeping baby.

"Merry Christmas!" they all shouted in return and stood on the stoop as the Howards carefully made their way down the steps to where the car was waiting.

CHAPTER 14

When Lord and Lady Linley finally arrived back at Highbury, the house was dark. The servants were no doubt still making merry somewhere in the bowels of the house, and thus Clive had to actually use his key to get in, something he hadn't had to do in ages—either here or in London. He pushed the heavy door open and escorted Henrietta and Teddy into the house.

"You go on up while I drive the car around back. I won't be long."

"Can't you just leave it in the drive?" Henrietta said wearily. "Albert or one of them can park it in the morning."

"Not in this cold. It'll never start again."

"All right, darling. I'll meet you upstairs. Be quiet when you come in, though." She nodded at the bundle in her arms.

Clive turned up the collar on his coat and charged back into the cold. It had been a long night, and he was anxious to relax upstairs in their sitting room and to give Henrietta her Christmas gift. He had enjoyed teasing her these past weeks, acting as though he hadn't the time or desire to shop, but he had in actuality brought something with him from London. He hoped she would like it.

He slipped into the Alfa and drove it round the back to the stables, where he easily guided it into one of the old horse stalls. He switched off the ignition and sat for a few seconds, his breath freezing in front of him as he reflected on the evening with the Von Harmons. It had been a pleasant but chaotic affair, though he supposed that was part of their charm. They were an unconventional family, to say the least, the perfect example of nouveau riche, and yet, Elsie and Gunther themselves seemed to have escaped the usual trappings that accompanied instant wealth. They were thoughtful and kind and generous—to a fault perhaps, he mused, suddenly recalling the image of Mr. Ferguson licking his plate.

After everything Clive had been through in the war, he had admittedly been leery at first of Elsie's involvement with a German immigrant, but Gunther, with his quiet ways and patient demeanor, had inadvertently won him over. Clive had quite enjoyed speaking with him, in fact, and could imagine them as friends had circumstances been different. Theirs was the life that he and Henrietta had wanted for themselves before his father and uncle had died, unexpectedly bequeathing a lordship and so much unwanted responsibility upon him.

Well, he thought, hauling himself out of the car, duty was duty, and that was that. Henrietta tried in her own way to make their life as "normal" as possible, another reason he so loved her. He banged the car door shut, his eye catching the giant crack in the plaster in the wall in front of him. He looked up at the rafters and the thick wooden joists, birds' nests sticking out every so often all down the line. He let out a deep sigh. Sidney was right. This whole thing should be knocked down. It's what he himself had wanted to do for a long time, but his father had been resistant to any kind of change, especially in his latter years. And now he was guilty of doing the very same thing—resisting change. And why? Because it was Sidney?

He switched off the stable lights and stepped back into the snowy night, his coat billowing about him. Sidney had devoted his life to first his father and now his mother, and to Highbury, too, Clive supposed, in many ways over the years.

As he approached the house, he was tempted to go in through the back, as it was closer, but he didn't wish to disrupt the servants' Christmas party. The lights were on in the kitchen, he observed, and he thought he could hear singing. He instead trudged around to the front of the house.

It had begun to snow again, large flakes floating down and illuminated in the moonlight. Clive's eyes looked beyond the house to where the woods stood, and he was suddenly transported to a very different Christmas Eve spent at the Front. He felt a pain in his chest at the memory of the pure white snow at St. Mihiel, stained red for miles with the blood of most of his company. It would have been oddly beautiful if not so horrific.

Suddenly his breath froze up in his chest, and he bent over, his hands on his knees, as he struggled to breathe. He remained that way for at least five full minutes, trying to regain control of his racing mind. Finally, he forced himself to stand upright. Despite the cold, a thin layer of sweat had broken out on his forehead and ran down his neck. He hated these "fits." They rendered him helpless, and he hated being this vulnerable. He made himself walk toward the front door. He would not let this spoil his Christmas Eve, he resolved through gritted teeth.

He stepped into the foyer, shut the door behind him, and leaned against it, his breathing still labored. He closed his eyes and tried to focus on Henrietta's face and then Teddy's. Eventually, he felt his rapid heartbeat slow, but at the sound of footsteps, he jumped, his heart racing again. His eyes shot open. There was a figure on the staircase. It was Sidney.

"Ah! You made it back," the older man said quietly, descending the rest of the stairs. He was dressed in a robe and slippers and had his hands casually in the robe pockets. "How'd it go?"

"Fine." Clive made himself speak. "Yes, fine." He tried to smile. "Everything okay, here?" he asked, nodding at Sidney's robe.

"Yes, yes. Your mother has a headache and wants an aspirin. I haven't the foggiest idea where it's kept, but I'm guessing somewhere in the vicinity of the kitchen." He smiled at him kindly for a few moments.

Clive stared back, wanting to say something, but he couldn't think of what.

"Well, Merry Christmas." Sidney patted Clive on the shoulder and turned to go.

Clive suddenly didn't want to be alone, but he didn't want to go upstairs just yet, either. He quickly calculated how long it would take Henrietta to get Teddy undressed, his diaper changed, a fresh nightgown put on, and probably another nursing . . .

"Tell you what," Clive called. "I'll get the aspirin if you pour us a quick drink. What do you say? For Christmas?"

Sidney closed one eye, likewise considering. "Yes, okay. A quick one. Study?"

Clive nodded and hurried toward the dining room. There was a passage there that led to the butler's pantry, where he knew various remedies were stashed by the staff, aspirin being one of them. The noise of the Christmas party coming from the kitchen was loud, which provided a perfect cover for Clive to gently open the glass cabinet doors and extract a bottle of aspirin tucked behind a silver coffee carafe along with various other tonics and pills. He gently shut the door behind him and strode quietly back to the study.

Sidney had already poured two brandies and handed him one. "Merry Christmas."

Clive set the bottle of aspirin on the desk and raised his glass, hoping Sidney wouldn't notice that his hand slightly shook. "Merry Christmas."

They both took a sip.

"Nice work about the gifts," Sidney said, taking a seat near the fireplace.

"Oh, that? Well, it wasn't exactly difficult." Clive leaned against the mantel, exceedingly glad to talk about something—anything—to banish the awful memories.

"What happened when you went to the Braithewaites'?" Sidney asked calmly. "You never said."

"Well, I'm supposed to be sworn to secrecy, but turns out the real thief was Beatrice Braithewaite, Victoria's daughter, who was helped, I should add, by that little rat Noland Peters."

"Really? But why?"

Clive felt himself relaxing back into the here and now and related the whole story to Sidney, who listened attentively.

"My God." Sidney took a deep drink. "I never did care much for Hugh. I wonder if Victoria suspects his philandering."

Clive shrugged. "It's Beatrice I feel sorry for." He walked absently toward the desk and was tempted to rifle through the papers sitting there but then caught himself, remembering that it wasn't his—or his father's—desk anymore. He let out a deep breath. "Look, Sidney . . . Sidney. I'm sorry I've been an ass lately."

"No need, Clive. You've already apologized. I understand."

Clive turned toward him. "I'm not sure you do. I . . . I *want* you to make changes to the place. You probably love Highbury more than I do." He shot Sidney a quick glance, and Sidney returned it with a small sad smile. "It's yours now. Do with it what you like. You and Mother. I'm happy for you both. Truly."

"Thank you, Clive. I'll still consult you on big issues."

"You don't need to. I trust you completely. I . . ." He looked down at the papers on the desk. "Truth is, I miss my father very much. And it's nice having you—" he broke off, unable to finish the sentiment. He cleared his throat. "So what was this business that Glenn alluded to?" he asked, forcing the emotion from his voice.

"Oh, that? Forget about it." Sidney stood and clapped him on the back. "We can discuss it in the coming days and not," he nodded at the clock, "on Christmas Eve when you have a lovely wife waiting for you upstairs and I am supposed to be locating aspirin." He reached for the bottle and slipped it into his robe pocket.

"True enough." Clive knocked back his brandy. "Merry Christmas, Sidney."

Sidney drained his glass as well. "Merry Christmas."

Clive hurried up the staircase and down the long hall to their wing, hoping, selfishly, that Teddy would be asleep. He slid open the pocket doors as quietly as he could and was pleased to see Henrietta curled up on the sofa in front of the fire. The room was bathed in darkness, save for the glow of the fire and two small table lamps. He tiptoed closer, and she turned and smiled at him. She was so utterly beautiful that he sometimes thought his heart would stop.

"All is well?" he asked softly, coming around and nodding toward the bedroom where Teddy's cradle was.

"Yes; he's finally asleep, hopefully for the night."

"You've changed," he said, noting that she was now wearing the brown plaid pants she had picked up at Bergdorf Goodman's when they docked in New York, a fashion item she had not yet dared to sport in front of Antonia, but one which Clive found oddly attractive in how daring they were. And she had removed her shoes and was wearing nothing but socks.

"Well, it's pretty hard, I discovered, to care for a baby whilst wearing a Chanel gown, darling. Especially the diapering part. *And* it had mashed potatoes on it."

Clive grinned. "Point taken." He began unraveling his tie. "Then let me get out of this. I won't be a moment." He strode quickly to his bedroom and went through to his dressing room.

"But, darling, shouldn't we be getting to bed?" Henrietta called softly after him. "It's dreadfully late. Teddy will be up early, and Edna's not here . . ."

Clive did not answer and instead hurriedly pulled off his evening suit and selected a pair of tweed trousers from the neatly hung assortment. Pascal, he noted, as he pulled on an oxford shirt and reached for a gray cable-knit sweater, was getting better and better. He unearthed two packages from one of his dresser drawers and hurried back out.

"But what about our gifts?" he said softly as he approached the sofa. "Are we not exchanging? It is Christmas Eve, you know."

Henrietta's face was one of surprise. "I assumed we'd wait until tomorrow."

"We didn't last year. And as that was our first Christmas together, so now it must be our tradition."

Henrietta suddenly let out a laugh and stood up. "You're so predictable, Inspector. I'm one step ahead of you." She gestured at the little tree in the corner, under which sat several gifts. "It seems that Santa has already been here. You missed him." She tapped his nose.

Clive slid his gifts onto a side table and wrapped his arms around her waist. "I'm not sure I like the idea of you being alone with another man up here," he grunted.

"Well, how do you know I was here when he came?" She smiled mischievously. "But as it happens, I was. And," she pursed her lips and raised her eyebrows, "he's not as old as one imagines. And he's really rather charming."

"Listen, Minx. I've had enough of lecherous old men preying on young women."

"Isn't that rather like the pot calling the kettle black?" she asked prettily.

Clive laughed. "How dare you!" His desire for her was rising, and he lowered his hands to her bottom.

"None of that, Inspector!" she said, removing his hands. She gave him a long, slow kiss, however, before she pulled away, which almost made it worse. "You pour us a drink, and I'll get your gift."

Clive ran a hand through his hair. "Yes, all right. Good idea. Sherry or cognac?"

"Oh, definitely cognac." She returned from the tree with a small package wrapped in shiny red paper. She placed it beside her on the sofa and took the glass he offered.

Clive sat next to her, still trying to dampen his arousal, and eyed the gift. In truth, he was intrigued to open it. Before he had met her, he had always received the same few gifts at Christmas from his parents and Julia—a random selection from the same assortment: embroidered handkerchiefs, cuff links, a tiepin, socks, a wallet, driving gloves, a watch.

In contrast to all of that, Henrietta had surprised him—nay astonished him—last year with an engraved sign for a detective agency that didn't yet—and now would never—exist. It was the most ridiculous gift he had ever received, but by the same token, his favorite. He couldn't imagine how she would top it this year and therefore tried to assume that she hadn't, that she had settled for something more traditional, say, a new tie. Still, he wondered . . .

"You first!" she said, thrusting the gift into his hands.

"You sure?" he asked, turning it over and over, trying to guess.

"Of course I am!"

Clive obeyed and gently ripped the paper to reveal a smooth brown box underneath. *Forester's* was embossed in gold across the lid. Forester's, he was pretty certain, was the haberdashery in town. She had gotten him a hat? But the box wasn't big enough for a hat. He lifted the lid and pulled back the tissue to reveal a houndstooth cap in the style of Sherlock Holmes. A deerstalker, he thought it was called. He laughed out loud as he lifted it from the box and examined it.

"I decided to stay with the theme, you see." Her eyes were delightfully bright with excitement. "There's more." She nodded at the box.

Clive set the cap down and rifled through the tissue to unearth a lovely pipe made of rosewood and ivory. He held it up and raised an eyebrow. "Let me venture a guess. This is meant to be Sherlock's pipe?"

"Yes!" Henrietta laughed. "Though I can't be certain it's the same. I was trying to remember the film."

Clive leaned over and kissed her. "Darling, this is an utterly ridiculous gift, but I love it. But why do you keep getting me detective things?"

"Because it's the one thing you don't have. It's a way to keep your dream alive."

"But, darling, it's not my dream. You are. And Teddy."

She picked up her cognac and took a sip, leaning back. "You don't fool me, Inspector. You were in your element these last few days."

"Put it down to a Christmas fantasy. Here," he placed a gift wrapped in simple brown paper in her hands.

She rubbed her fingers along the edge. "It feels like a book," she declared.

"That's because it *is* a book. The question is which one?"

"Spoil sport!" She gave his arm a little pinch, which he found delightful. She tore open the paper, and as she examined the book in her hands, her face went from one of amusement to one of deep appreciation.

"Clive! I don't think I have this one."

"Probably not. Not this *particular* one, at any rate. It's a first edition of her first work. And," he smiled, "it's signed by the author." He leaned his head against his fist, propped up on the cushions on the back of the sofa, utterly enjoying watching her delight.

"Oh, my!" Henrietta quickly opened *The Mysterious Affair at Styles* and saw *Agatha Christie* scrawled across the first page. "Where did you get this?"

"In a little shop in London. Old and rare books, that sort of thing."

"You brought it all this way?"

He grinned.

"Oh, Clive! It's wonderful." She leaned toward him and kissed him. "Oh, I'm sorry I didn't get you something better."

"Better? What could be finer?" He reached for the cap and put it on and thrust the pipe between his lips. They both laughed. "Well, the pipe will come in handy," he said, examining the pipe closer as he pulled off the cap.

"But what is that?" Henrietta nodded toward the long thin gift still on the side table.

Clive reached for it. "This," he said, holding it up, "is for my son."

"Oh, Clive! So, you *did* get him something."

"Of course I did. It's my cricket bat from school," he said reverently.

Henrietta surprised him by laughing. "A cricket bat? Isn't he a little young?"

"He'll grow into it," Clive said with a smile, putting the pipe back in his mouth, realizing that perhaps a cricket bat was a bit of a silly gift for a baby.

"Here, I'll put it with the other gifts for him from Santa. Or I suppose I should start calling him Father Christmas." She took the package from him and placed it carefully under the tree where several other gifts sat. Clive joined her.

"What did you get him? Seems a lot, don't you think?"

"Well, the nursery at home is rather bare, Clive. He needs *some* things to play with. Santa has brought him a train, a ball, a rattle, a toy horse, and a teddy bear," she said, pointing to each gift in turn.

"I suppose that's all right." Clive slipped his hand around her waist, and they stood admiring the gifts and the tree, his heart so full of joy and contentment he could barely stand it.

"Come," she said finally, "let's look for the Christmas star." She took his hand and pulled him toward the tall windows.

"The Christmas star?"

"Yes, didn't you do that as a kid? Look for the Christmas star?"

Clive grinned. "No."

Henrietta pulled back the thick damask curtain. The snow had stopped and lay glistening below. Clive avoided looking down at it, not wanting to resurrect his "fit," and instead searched the sky. His eyes strayed to Henrietta, then, and he drank in the sight of her, a tonic to his damaged soul, as she peered into the heavens as if she were actually looking for the Christmas star. She was so lovely, her features outlined beautifully in the moonlight. He felt he could gaze at her all night . . .

"There it is," she said, breaking his reverie and pointing indiscriminately. "Do you see it?"

Clive pulled back the curtain on his side and tried following her finger through the millions of stars arrayed across the sky and thought he *might* see one that was twinkling a little bit brighter. "Yes, I think so."

Henrietta pinched him again. "No, you don't!"

Clive laughed and put his free arm around her again, pulling her close. "It doesn't matter if I see it or not. You do, and that's all that matters. *You're* all that matters, Henrietta," he said hoarsely. "You and Teddy. He kissed the top of her head, and she wrapped her arms around him, laying her head on his chest. "I love you."

"I love you, too, Inspector," she said softly. "Merry Christmas."

"Merry Christmas, my love," he whispered and let the curtain fall.

ACKNOWLEDGEMENTS

Stepping back into Clive and Henrietta's world was enormously fun, and I hope you've enjoyed transporting back to the 1930s with me. This is the first Clive and Henrietta novel that I've produced independently, though to say that isn't really accurate. There is a lot that goes into the making of a book besides the writing, and I'm grateful to the little team I'm assembling around me to help me do just that.

First and foremost, I'd like to thank my new cover designer, Kari Brownlie (who is also designing the Merriweather Novels), for her brilliant vision of the new look of the Henrietta and Inspector Howard series. I admire Kari for the care and thought she puts into every project. Not only does she read the whole manuscript herself in order to capture a book's essence (unheard of!), but she brings her vast knowledge of publishing trends to the project as well. A book is only as good as its cover, and Kari has hit this one out of the park.

I'd also like to thank Susie Chinisci for editing and keeping track of the whole series for me. With each new book, more characters join the set, and Susie organizes them all into a neat and tidy story bible should my memory fail regarding the small details, which it quite often does. I admit, for example, that I find it hard to remember the makes and models of the many cars Alcott has parked in the Highbury stables, the name of the junior footman or the maid at Castle Linley, or the exact ages of any of the Von Harmon children at any given moment. Without Susie, I would be lost! Likewise, a big thank you to Danna Steele for her beautiful interior, and Bill Courtney for proofreading. Danna creates the bones of the book, and Bill makes sure everything is perfect and polished.

I'd also like to give a special shout-out to my sister, Marcy Martino, for her expert advice regarding the ever-popular Christmas novella. Having never read a Christmas novella myself, I relied heavily on Marcy's guidance and knowledge of this festive genre. I must say, I enjoyed writing a Christmas caper, and it has definitely sparked ideas for future episodes! I hope this first endeavor meets all the criteria for a cozy holiday read. Thank you, Marcy, for your help and suggestions!

And thanks, as always, to my husband, Phil, for standing by me, supporting me, listening to my latest crazy idea, and, in general, just letting me get on with it. Your faith in me is a true gift, and I would not be where I am on this journey but for you.

Lastly, I'd like to thank all of YOU for reading my books and for your encouraging support. YOU are why I continue to trudge along on this path, as any sane person would have abandoned ship long ago. Thank you for continuing to cheer me on and for your many kind comments. They are truly what keep me going.

And so there seems nothing left to say but to wish all of you a very merry Christmas! May the Spirit of the season wrap you up and hold you close in faith, hope, and, most especially, love, and may you have a happy, healthy, joyous New Year!

MORE FROM MICHELLE COX

The Henrietta and Inspector Howard Series

If this is your first engagement with Henrietta and Clive, you might want to dive into the main series. **The Henrietta and Inspector Howard series**, set in Chicago and abroad in the 1930s, has received over eighty international awards and reviews from *Library Journal* (starred), *Booklist* (starred), *Kirkus Reviews*, Historical Novel Society, *Redbook*, *Elle*, and many, many others.

"Henrietta and Inspector Howard make a charming odd couple, mixing mystery and romance in a fizzy 1930s cocktail."
—**Hallie Ephron,** *New York Times* best-selling author

"Brimming with dark plot on every page, this unpredictable literary thrill ride will transport you to the heart of 1930s Chicago and the love story of a lifetime."
—**POPSUGAR**

"Henrietta and Clive are a sexy, endearing, and downright fun pair of sleuths. Readers will not see the final twist coming."
—*Library Journal* (starred review)

Start the series for free!

The Merriweather Novels

The Merriweather Novels is a fun spin-off series of the Henrietta and Inspector Howard series. Set in small-town Wisconsin in the 1930s, it features Melody Merriweather (a minor character in the original series) and an all-new cast of characters. And, bonus—each book of the series is a Jane Austen retelling!

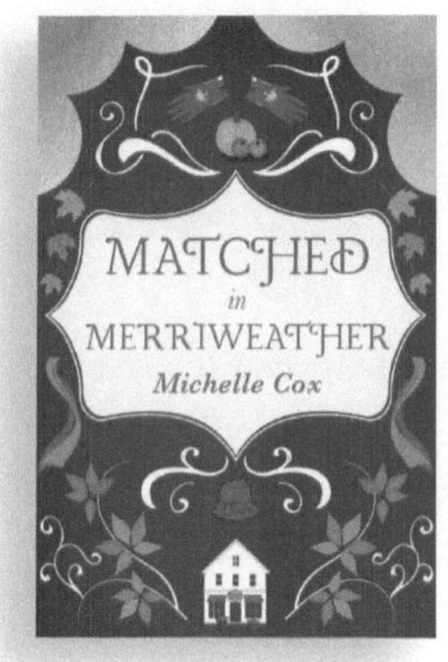

Try Book One, *Matched in Merriweather*, today!

The Fallen Woman's Daughter

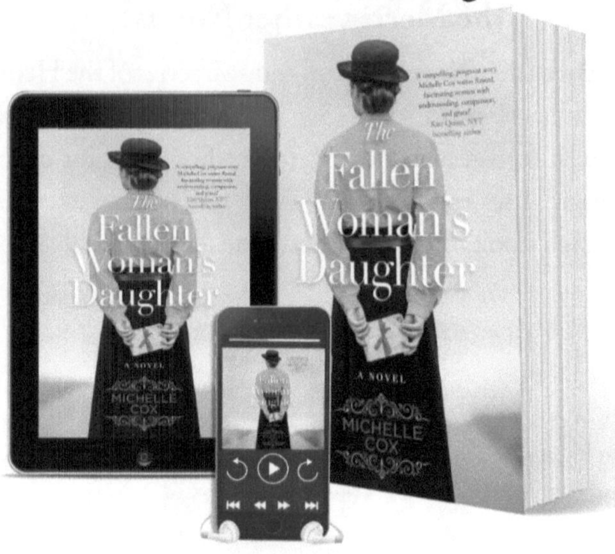

The Fallen Woman's Daughter is a stand-alone historical fiction novel based on the true story of a young girl from the coal-mining region of Southern Iowa who runs away with a carnival barker who comes through town. A story spanning forty years, this one will grab you and won't let go!

"Michelle Cox writes flawed, fascinating women with understanding, compassion, and grace—I rooted for them with every turn of the page!"
—**Kate Quinn,** *New York Times* best-selling author

Stay Connected to Michelle!

Meanwhile, stop by Michelle's website and sign up for her news-letter at michellecoxauthor.com/newsletter-signup/ or scan the QR code below for alerts about new releases, free stuff, events, and fabulous giveaways! She always has something fun going on!